CHRISTIANA SPENS is the author of several books including *Shooting Hipsters: Rethinking Dissent in the Age of PR* (Repeater Books, 2016), *The Portrayal and Punishment of Terrorists in Western Media: Playing the Villain* (Palgrave Macmillan, 2019) and *The Fear* (Repeater Books, 2023). She also writes regularly for publications such as *The New Statesman*, *The Irish Times*, *Glamour*, *Stylist*, *Literary Hub*, *The London Magazine*, *Prospect* and *Studio International* on culture, psychology and politics, and sometimes works as an illustrator for books by Granta, NYRB, and other publishers.

Also by Christiana Spens

The Fear (Repeater Books, 2023)
The Portrayal and Punishment of Terrorists in Western Media: Playing the Villain (Palgrave Macmillan, 2019)
Shooting Hipsters: Rethinking Dissent in the Age of PR (Repeater Books, 2016)

The Colony

CHRISTIANA SPENS

CROMER

PUBLISHED BY SALT PUBLISHING 2026

2 4 6 8 10 9 7 5 3 1

Copyright © Christiana Spens 2026

Christiana Spens has asserted her right under the Copyright, Designs
and Patents Act 1988 to be identified as the author of this work.

*This book is sold subject to the condition that it shall not, by way of trade or otherwise,
be lent, resold, hired out, or otherwise circulated without the publisher's prior consent
in any form of binding or cover other than that in which it is published and without a
similar condition including this condition being imposed on the subsequent publisher.*

This book is a work of fiction. Any references to historical events, real people
or real places are used fictitiously. Other names, characters, places and events
are products of the author's imagination, and any resemblance to actual
events or places or persons, living or dead, is entirely coincidental.

First published in Great Britain in 2026 by
Salt Publishing Ltd
12 Norwich Road, Cromer NR27 0AX United Kingdom

www.saltpublishing.com

Salt Publishing Limited Reg. No. 5293401

A CIP catalogue record for this book is available from the British Library

ISBN 978 1 78463 373 8 (Paperback edition)
ISBN 978 1 78463 374 5 (Electronic edition)

Typeset in Neacademia by Salt Publishing

Printed and bound in Great Britain by Clays Ltd, Elcograf S.p.A

With thanks to Caspian, who accompanied me on a trip to the island where I would realise how to finish this story.

'It's more useful for my mistakes to ripen and burst in their own good time.'

—PHILIP ROTH

'You would say, I should have been superior to circumstances; so I should – so I should; but you see I was not. When fate wronged me, I had not the wisdom to remain cool: I turned desperate; then I degenerated.'

—*Jane Eyre*, CHARLOTTE BRONTE

'Let us swear an oath, and keep it with an equal mind,
in the hollow Lotos-land to live and lie reclined
On the hills like Gods together, careless of mankind.'

—'The Lotos-Eaters', TENNYSON

The Colony

1

I WAS ALWAYS convinced that I would never meet anyone ever again, that when one relationship was over, it was all over. There was no future; without some man to dwell on, the future itself just didn't exist. And yet the men kept coming, so this existential terror was never really tested. What would happen if there were no more men? I never found out.

And yet the pain did not diminish. On this occasion, I was sitting in the jacuzzi of a spa my most recent boyfriend had booked me into to help me feel better about our breaking up. It was just me and another couple, and we had an unspoken agreement not to use the jacuzzi at the same time. I got there first, so I was in the jacuzzi - very sullen but trying to make the best of the situation - while they were in the steam room. They had been in there twenty minutes, and I knew they wouldn't come out until I left the jacuzzi. Briefly, I enjoyed this sad power, but it did little to pierce the overwhelming tedium of my pain. I was taking my time. I was wondering how long it would take until my ex took another girl here, and then they would be the couple. And then perhaps they would be forced into the steam room for an uncomfortable stretch of time, by someone like me.

The flow of bubbles ended, so once again I pressed the green button and it started up again, and the couple remained in there, in their white sweaty tank, talking about their work, and when the woman was once unemployed, and waiting for me to grow tired of this. I closed my eyes and remembered the last time we were together, how for the briefest moment I knew it was the last time, it must be the last, because nothing this good ever lasts. Knowing it can't last is what makes it so good. And that is what had made it last this long.

But knowing it can't last gradually turns every other moment into a painful stretch – just waiting, always waiting, until no climax will hide the imminent death; no more a little death but an endless, nagging one. 'I'm so lucky,' I had thought then, as he put his clothes back on, as I sat there naked still, unable to get up, unwilling to try. He left the room. Now I opened my eyes. He was not here, never would have been here. I had spent my winnings, I spent them as I won them. The cycle ended, the bubbles stopped, and the room was bathed in a pink, hellish glow. I had been here before, this amniotic swell. I waited to be born again, I made my maker wait, I punished myself, too, with the fear of separation.

I remembered him as a soft, blue weight I never wanted to be released from; this foolish, heavy devotion was imprinted in me. My body waited for that same weight after he had gone, a numbed, blissful sense of weight, which was technically impossible. It was a dreamt thing, a levitation. I waited for it nevertheless, for something impossible. Softness and height and a particular body. A fantasy.

When we first met, he said, 'Nothing should ever happen between us.' It would be a disaster, he assured me. And yet this triggered some compulsion in me, as perhaps he knew it would; the more we seemed to be doomed, the more I wanted him. It infuriated me that I was repeating myself in this obvious and foolish way, that I had found someone who was, I thought at times, an amalgamation of every other past boyfriend. But I liked being around him; or rather, as time went on, our mutual disappearance. When he faded from reality, I faded with him. When he smoked, I smoked too, sharing his sweet and poisoned air. And yet there was no air left now, and he was gone too, and when I awoke the following day, I knew it was all over. I lay there for some time, letting everything else I had slip away, craving things I could not have, with some feeling that if I waited long enough, I would be found.

※

I was getting the impression that the therapist was becoming frustrated with me. I had been telling her about all my past relationships, and how they had been one repeat after another of that first damaging one with Tristan, and how frustrating it was for me, to be repeating myself in this manner.

'Well, why do you always choose the same person, more or less?'

We had had this conversation before, as well; now, even the therapy was repeating itself. 'I suppose it's a compulsion,' I said. 'Though it's genuinely unconscious; even when I can see what is happening, I still can't stop myself. I can't resist, in those moments, and then before long it is too late, and I'm in this vortex.' I was irritated at the stupidity of it as I remembered it. 'All my friends warned me off him,' I went on, talking not about Tristan but the most recent boyfriend. 'Complete strangers warned me off him. But I just liked him immediately. He had a look, and I didn't want it to leave me.'

'Did the fact you were told not to go near him add to the allure, perhaps?' I smiled, remembered, indulged.

'I suppose so. It seemed to me that I really couldn't say no. I couldn't not go along with it. It overpowered me. I couldn't say no. And neither could he. And I liked that about him.'

'And that must have been exciting?' she replied, wearily.

'Yes; until it was torturous. But I'm still sad it is over.' I remembered the sickness I felt, towards the end, when I saw his face on my phone. 'But also relieved.' I added. And then I remembered when I would actually see him, and I felt only warmth and love, regardless of what had happened. 'And confusion,' I said. 'I was always confused and I still am. I am always confused.'

She sighed, but barely moved her face. She was sitting in a poised way, wearing cream-coloured glasses, her hands neatly in her lap. She must see this all the time, I thought. She just nodded, ever so slightly, as if she could hear me psychically as well. 'It all feels very impersonal, though,' I went on, talking about not just this man, but therapy too. 'Trying to connect feels futile now. It is hard not to feel defeated.'

I saw her look at the clock on the table, which faced her and not me, so I didn't know what time it was. I paused. 'Are we almost out of time?' I asked.

'Almost,' she said. 'But we can talk more about this next week. Perhaps you might think about why it is that you find it hard to connect.'

'Okay. Thanks,' I said, and I got up, gathered my things. I was exhausted, I kept thinking, all the time, every day. I am exhausted. I have no feelings left because I am just always like this. As I walked out of the building, past the waiting room where a few others were sitting, I thought about what I did not talk about in therapy, but nearly raised, that he had also said he could not connect to me anymore. That I would not let him in. I had been upset when he said this; I had been trying so hard, I said, as he looked at me furiously. 'You're not capable of it,' he said. 'There's no point, you're not capable of it.'

Later, he raised the subject of sleeping pills and Xanax again, but I had dismissed this, doubled down on how much I had been trying lately. I doubted he really cared anyway; it seemed more likely he was using that problem to deflect from his own recent behaviour. If he could not get through to me, it was only because my defences were up, after everything that had happened lately, and yet he told me this was some failure on my part.

'But it's impossible to let you in, to talk to you,' I replied, 'if I feel like there's a gun to my head. You don't listen to me; you just keep forcing me to say things, but I have no idea what you're asking of me anymore. I'm telling you everything, and it is never enough. I told you everything.'

He was still furious, though; he was giving up on me. It didn't matter what I said.

'I'm sorry,' he said, and I knew he was leaving, had already found someone else, had been gone sometime already.

※

There was some truth in what he had said about the sleeping pills, but at the time it seemed an unfair thing to dwell on, when I had given up alcohol for some time, and the reason I couldn't sleep was, at least partly, due to the anxiety he had inspired in me. But with him gone, and having to face that sense of abandonment afresh, it only grew worse. And while he may have triggered the most recent problems, I had been a bad sleeper before as well, and this medicating myself to sleep, which he had enabled after all, seemed an obvious solution. But over time I could not imagine life without some chemical crutch; I could not believe I would ever sleep alone. I wanted an everyday oblivion; something if not someone to soothe me to sleep; the soft blow to the head, of a small white bullet, a tablet on my tongue.

I tried to imagine a life free of this dependency, but it seemed absurd to me the more I considered it. Why give up something so soft and enveloping? It was like a prayer lingering into the night, a soft-sweet glow, an amber haze that lulled me into a fleeting peace. Why give up that easy height, a slowing breath, those glowing, easy thoughts? I could not imagine life without it, just as I could not imagine life without sleep or dreams or the distant promise of death. He had brought it to my night against the brutal dark of his days, and so this would be mine, now. He had medicated the wounds he made, I let him play doctor. I kept playing without him.

And yet even alone, I remembered these moments with him: how my heart quickened and then slowed under his influence. How I had tumbled down his stairs and only felt how soft the material of the carpet was, how mellow his voice. I remembered how the doorbell seemed to become a flute in harmony with his voice, but it was just his dealer arriving and leaving again, or his mother calling. My voice sounded different, too; love seemed to echo in every sensation, in the lamp my eyes rested on, in the piano of another song, my fingers feeling each note, cool as marble keys, cool as him.

I made resolutions to change, but with each attempt, I couldn't let go. I didn't want to feel grief or separation, and I accepted and desired numbness so long as it prevented that worse pain. I would rather I disappear than he disappeared; or at least I acted that way. He was a tornado I preferred to be at the centre of for as long as I could be, rather than detritus left in his wake.

I never considered there was a chance I might not need some kind of oblivion, or even that being sleepless or sleep deprived, or in my own company, was not the worst thing on earth. But I think I knew that if I stopped taking them, stopped desiring some version of him, stopped medicating myself, then I would have to live the reality of it all fully, and I would have to acknowledge the relationship, and all it left in its wake, was intolerable.

Although it was over now, and I had moved out of our apartment entirely, my thoughts always drifted back, so it was as if I were still there. I remembered how he passed out on the floor on his birthday and wouldn't wake. How I pulled him to his bedroom and made him comfortable on the floor. How I lay with him there, fell asleep until he woke me with his nightmares. He clamped around me, then; I settled him like a child. Eventually it passed. In the morning, he ate some of the birthday cake I had bought him: with passion fruit and syrup, vanilla mousse. I made coffee and sat with him as it started over again. Later, he fell asleep in my arms.

I missed the closeness of being in such a bad place together, I think; I lay awake at night, unable to sleep, wishing I could be transported back there for a moment. He allowed this excess from me, demanded mad devotion. And I gave it unthinkingly, and that was on me, now that it was all over. Even without someone to love, my body seemed to wait for it, unable even to sleep alone. If I had not already recognised this as a dependency, now I did. I had loved the shadow side too much; I only ended up finding parallel routes to misery, repeating the histories of those I loved, falling into the mirror they held up, drowning in a reflection that became mine.

At a loss, in this moment of loneliness, I phoned my old friend Nate, whom I knew would not be fazed, would not be judgemental. 'Oh Lena,' he said, though he did not sound all that surprised. 'Come round, we'll sort something out. You don't have to be in these terrible co-dependent relationships anymore,' he said. 'But you might need a bit of help.'

※

I arrived at Nate's favourite coffee shop at 2 p.m. in Stoke Newington the next day, and he greeted me warmly, standing up from his table at the back to kiss me on the cheek. He was wearing loose black trousers and a warm grey tee-shirt that said Fairport Convention, his hair quite long these days, curling around his ears, and he was looking well. He ordered us a pot of coffee to share, and I told him what had happened, how bad things had got. He had mentioned the retreat before, but I had never had the time. But now I had nothing else.

'You need a fresh start,' Nate said. 'Or this will consume you.

It's either AA meetings or the island, and I know which one I prefer.' The retreat offered a combination of painting classes and wellness sessions. He invited various people to take part – sound healers, yogis, shamans, therapists, an open-minded Priest. It was a little, windswept utopia, his passion project, a long-running installation on a rock in the North Sea.

'I can't afford it,' I replied. 'I would have gone before if I could have.'

'You never would have left him; that's the real reason.' He said knowingly, which felt comforting to me. 'But don't worry about the money. You can help me run the place, even things out. It'll be good for you.' And so that is how the decision was made, in the dreary wasteland of one more bad relationship. He took my hand, and though I had resisted the idea before, it seemed at last to be the right time.

He would lead the way, he would save me from the latest disaster, from my own cascade of bad decisions. He would take me to Gull Island, where the Monks and then Vikings had been before, he said, where only birds lived in the centuries since, and we would mend ourselves at last.

2

THAT FRIDAY, WE took the train up to Leuchars in Fife, and then a bus to the coast. I brought an overnight bag and left the rest in storage. I had just brought some clothes and a few books, my Olympus Trip, and a few rolls of film. The trip up was long but pleasant; Nate gave me the window seat so that as we got further north, and the landscapes more rugged and sublime, I could see them more clearly. The sea seemed to become a deeper indigo the further up we went, the stretches between towns and cities greater, the houses further apart.

I had grown up further down the coast, south of Edinburgh, but only until I was nine, when my father died, and my mother moved us to London where her family lived. Since then, I had lived in Glasgow with my ex, but I had only returned once to the East Coast, for the Edinburgh Festival, and I had not been paying much attention to the landscape back then.

I felt idiotic now, to have not seen what was there all along, to have not known I had been craving it without realising it, especially when Nate had been gently turning me that way for years. He was a landscape painter, after all; he had gone to the Slade the same time I had gone to Goldsmiths for photography, and all the time he had been running retreats on the island, he had been producing these beautiful works. And yet I had been blind to it all, immersed in my smaller world.

As we passed Edinburgh, with about an hour left to go, I asked Nate more about the island. 'It's somewhere between an artists' retreat and a rehab, I suppose. But we're not overly strict; people take their time and forge their own path. But any drink is rationed, and you won't find much else, so you will need to adapt. And if it all gets too much, you can always leave.' I felt nervous as he said this, and yet I was not an addict per se, I told myself; I had no daily need for anything except sleeping pills, and I had mostly stopped taking them. Nevertheless, the realisation I would have no easy access concerned me, or perhaps more so, that access was in the control of other people I had never met.

'So, who organises all that – the medication, the food, the logistics?'

He smiled dismissively. 'Don't worry, we won't let you starve, or even suffer. There are regular boats back and forth from the island, and we have the essentials stockpiled. We get deliveries from our fishermen and research friends sometimes as well.'

'Researchers?'

'For the birds,' he said. 'There are scientists who have to keep track of what the birds are doing. It's their island, really. We're just guests there. If there are any important sightings – like whales, for instance – then we keep them updated. We've only seen one this summer though,' he said, seeming to remember it wistfully. 'They're quite rare.'

With that, I started daydreaming about whales and puffins, too, rather than worrying about potential insomnia and anxiety. 'You'll feel a lot better on the island anyway,' he went on. 'All the sea air, being outside all the time. It can be transformative.' I looked out of the window again as he went back to his music and lost myself in the passing fields and woods, hoping he would be right.

When we arrived in Leuchars, a grey haze had descended, though it was not quite raining yet. I followed Nate over the bridge towards a bus shelter, and we waited until one drew up. Then we sat together at the back, tired now, and listened to our own music as we drove past an RAF base, then a distillery, then farmland. Eventually we arrived in St. Andrews, and got another bus, to take us further down the coast.

It was getting dark by now and I was sleepy, and Nate seemed exhausted too. But we arrived in Anstruther before nightfall, though after that day's boat to the island had set off. 'We can stay at this B&B,' he explained, when we arrived, 'but let's have something to eat first. I'm starving, and you must be too. There is a place round here that does the best fish and chips, if the queue isn't too bad this time. Sometimes it winds all around the building, but it's worth it.'

I was hoping that would not be the case, after eight hours of traveling already, and thankfully it was not too bad. In front of us, a group of policemen were standing in line, waiting for their fish suppers. 'They've had a hard day fighting crime,' Nate deadpanned, and yet I noticed he avoided eye contact all the same.

After we got our food, we went to a little beach to the left of the harbour, where the tide was out, and we sat down together on the sand, leaning against our bags. 'I've never been so hungry in my life,' I said, realising only as I ate that I had been starving all day.

'Well enjoy it,' Nate said, meanly I thought. 'No fish and chips on the island.'

'There must be some fish, at least?'

He smiled, and though I wondered if we would be fishing, I just continued eating rather than asking more questions.

After that, we booked into a small B&B that was only yards away from where the boat would depart the next day. I was in a twin room with Nate, decorated in the generic seaside town décor I had seen in the B&Bs of Margate, Hastings, Brighton – blue and white stripes, sentimental framed pictures of shells and sea-birds.

I unpacked a few things while Nate had a shower, emerging in a cloud of steam and a small white towel minutes later.

'Is there a bath?' I asked, since I hadn't been into the bathroom yet. He swanned past me, laying down on his bed with his eyes closed, steam escaping through the open window to his right.

'There is, yes. Enjoy it while you can,' he said again. 'No baths on the island.'

'I get the point,' I replied, taking my jeans off and grabbing the shampoo I had brought with me. 'What is on the island? Are there showers at least?'

He broke into a grin, though his eyes were still closed. 'There are showers, they're just not always very warm. But it's nice to swim in the sea, anyway. You'll like it.'

Though I began to find it presumptuous that he might know what I'd like, I went into the bathroom and started running the water, determined to enjoy all the warmth that I could before we set off.

The following day, we were up quite early, taking breakfast in the B&B's crowded breakfast room with some American and German tourists who barely spoke. I drank three cups of black coffee, eggs, bacon, sausages, and toast; this time, Nate did not have to tell me to enjoy the food as if I were on death row, and I went ahead and filled my plate without prompting.

Our boat was scheduled to leave at 10.30 a.m., so we had to be at the harbour for 9.45, standing with our bags as the boat bobbed in the water. It was overcast now, and though relatively calm, when we boarded, we sat in the enclosed section, on seats at the front of the boat. As we waited for the others to board - a few researchers who were running late - I looked at all the boats bobbing gently in the harbour, knocking against one another, their colours and signs mirrored in the glistening water.

Though I had been increasingly nervous about the decision

to go to the retreat, as the boat left the harbour, and seeing the lighthouse disappear behind us, until I could see nothing around us but the glimmering sea, I felt the expanse of freedom that Nate had been promising. For an hour, I just gazed out the window, taken by the ocean that wrapped around us, forgetting everything I had left behind, as if in a trance.

After about an hour, I caught a glimpse of the island at last; though I had seen it from the mainland before, now it grew nearer and nearer, formidable with its sheer cliff faces and deep granite rock. It was a severe and beautiful thing. I took some photographs, and then turned back to Nate.

'Thank you for taking me here,' I said.

'We haven't even arrived yet! But you're welcome. It's my pleasure. It's always nice to see a new person find it for the first time.' In that moment, I remembered how we had first met – at a mutual friend's funeral in Soho – and it seemed miraculous that now we were here together, ten years later.

'It's exactly what I need, I think. I already feel better, just being away from everything.'

'That's the main thing,' he replied, rooting through his backpack for his water bottle. 'It's the physical distance. It's hard to go no contact if you know you could bump into them at a party or something. But here – and you should delete your socials too, by the way – you can rest easy, because you know that won't happen.'

'I just wish I'd never been with him,' I said, though this wasn't exactly true. I wanted to feel that repelled but the truth was that I missed him, felt quite attached to memories of happier times.

'I feel bad I introduced you,' Nate said. I had been visiting him in Glasgow when we had met Aidan in a pub one night and we had struck up a conversation.

'You weren't to know,' I replied. 'And you barely introduced us. In fact, I think you even warned me off him.'

'Yes, but I should have known that would only make you want him more. It was inevitable.'

'How's the painting going?' I asked, trying to change the subject.

'Pretty well actually,' he said. 'I have a little studio on the island, a few commissions. You can help me with that maybe; that can help pay for your board.'

I smiled, bemused by this old-fashioned arrangement. He had created a fantasy here. 'Sure.' I replied, all the same.

'Everyone pitches in really,' he went on. 'It's like a little village. We have to be very careful with food, plan everything in advance. We look after the building, the studio. We contribute to research on the birds, noting sightings, that sort of thing. We are guests on the island, and we behave accordingly.'

'Understood.'

Nate told me more about who was on the island at that moment: Adrian, who organised most of the wellness classes, Hana, his girlfriend who was also a painter; Sacha, a recovering ketamine addict turned sound healer, and the Priest, otherwise known as Jon, who kept an open mind. There were others, too, whose names escaped me, who drifted back and forth. Nate himself was 'mostly sober' these days, he said, having given up everything for a year and then incrementally allowed himself little rations of old pleasures.

'We take a kind approach to sobriety on the island,' he explained, when I betrayed my own confusion about the set-up. 'It is not just all or nothing; we accept you at every stage of recovery. But for you, in this moment, it would probably be best to be abstinent, until you recover. I think in your case, your issue is your relationships, anyway. All starting with Tristan, of course.' He looked uneasy as he said this, then looked ahead at the island on the horizon. 'You need to give up a certain type of relationship before you can give up the other bad habits; they are just symptoms of the original problem. I think it's kind of fateful we have ended up here though. We met at his funeral, and now finally, all these years later, you are in the right place. We met so that you could be here now. I do believe that.' He said this with such a sweet certainty, that I believed it too.

Moments later, the boat pulled into the harbour, which was really just a small dock, where colonies of gulls welcoming us as they perched on their dappled grey rocks. This was their island, I remembered again, Nate's voice gradually drowned out by their cries. Our colony could not disturb theirs.

It was only as Nate climbed onto the deck and then down a ramp onto the dock that I realised he was carrying an extra bag very carefully, and the birds seemed to notice too, swarming around him, and squawking to each other with shrill cries. He ducked down, laughing, beckoning me to follow.

'I can't keep a secret on this island,' he said. 'It's the oysters they're after, I swear they can smell them on me. The oysters and the crab, their favourite, but also mine.' I hadn't seen him buy them; the birds had given away his surprise.

'And mine,' I said, and he turned with a smile, batting the gulls away. 'They're my favourite too.'

'Let's go then, come on. Before the birds get ideas.'

I walked on behind him, as he led the way, a wave of adoration sweeping over me. As I looked around, not only the beauty of the place but its sheer isolation exhilarated me; and I had Nate to thank for that. He had brought me here; he had brought me out of a small little world to this soaring expanse; and he had brought oysters, too.

As I followed him a slight regret passed over me though; I wished I had not been diverted from him the way that I had all my life so far; I wished we had met some other way than at a funeral. I wished I had come here sooner, been here with him decades ago. If only I had known him a little earlier, I thought, as children perhaps, if we had met then, then maybe life would have worked out differently. If only I had not gone chasing other people, entranced by other places, if only I had not got so lost.

But perhaps I would have ended up on this island either way, the ever-evasive home I missed before I knew it, much like Nate himself, and the man who had inadvertently brought us together all those years ago.

3

LONDON, 2012

I FIRST MET Tristan when I was nineteen, though I looked a lot younger, so he said. I had just moved to London; I'd been there a week. He was in his early forties and had a reputation, to the extent that I'd been warned off him by my editor already – the drugs, the prostitutes, especially – and yet, somehow, this only added to the intrigue. He had a record out; it was mainly about heroin, love, and death. It was what interested me, then. Two in the afternoon, he had said. Come round. We'll have a chat.

I knew the face, the gaze, I knew it as if we had met before, but we hadn't. I had seen his face on a press release, but that was all. As I climbed up the stairs, he opened a door.

'Hello.' he said, looming over me. And I became someone else, just like that, with a certain look. I smiled. We played the same game. We danced in each other's reflections. We used one another, like dark pools with the endless depths of our own sadness, curiosity, how far we could go. We played the same game and yet I had never played before, I would be defeated. On some level, I must have known this, and yet I kept playing.

We talked about his music and recent interviews, in which he said he had cleaned up, rid his life of demons, found some sense of peace without self-medication. I thought that sounded admirable, aspirational, even. I had tried three sorts of antidepressants that year, and none of them had worked. I wanted guidance from someone who understood, and he was intriguing in this way; he had a story to tell. He was a story to tell. He taught that pain could be fashioned into prose, need not be wasted. My pain, by extension, could be material rather than a cross to bear. I liked this idea; it felt like a plan. It felt like a good enough way to live.

His flat had wooden floorboards smudged with paint and black rubber marks, and shelves of skulls above a fireplace. He sat at his desk to the right of it, by a collection of books – essays on Francis Bacon and the Romantic poets. There were pictures on the wall, mostly of himself. He sat in black trousers and a torn black cashmere sweater; he looked at me with a mischievous smile. Sad and defiant dark brown eyes. Attention, unwavering. When was the last time someone had looked at me like that? When had anyone ever looked at me like that?

'Is it alright if I smoke in here?' I asked, sitting on a red velvet window seat. 'If I open the window?'

'Course,' he said, and I pushed it open. I lit a cigarette, glanced out at the cobbled street below – a tailor's just steps away, an Indian restaurant to the left. I relaxed into the seat, the smoke, this male's gaze.

'What do you do, when you're not doing music?' I asked him.

'Girls, smack, and painting. Well, not painting. Or much music, for that matter.'

'I thought you'd given up?' I asked. That was what he had said in his stories to the press and in his songs – his redemption, his happy ending. He was supposed to be eighteen months clean.

'I have. I have. I've given up.' His voice lilted as he smiled his sad smile again; I stubbed my cigarette into a heavy silver ashtray that he now handed over to me. He looked at me as if I were a child and it soothed me. Something soft, affectionate, primally desired. A glance that unfolded a need, a need that could not, had never been met. And it was too late now, at nineteen; it was time for simulations, perversions, replacements, substitutions. Bad habits all begin at once.

Then he turned away, morosely, though there was no obvious reason for it. And what was this – I felt sorry for him? Already? Puppy dog eyes on a grown man. Some kind of ache, things that I felt, projected back. I didn't want to feel sorry for myself anymore; so here was someone else's sad, unspoken story to feel instead. He didn't want to lose himself again; so here was someone else to watch dive head first into disaster.

'But you haven't given up yet, have you?' he asked. 'Let's go for a drink. I'm not drinking, but you can. I can get vicarious pleasure from watching you drink.' I picked up my jacket and bag and followed him unthinkingly.

'Where are we going?'

'The Colony Rooms.'

The club was just around the corner. The walls were painted a bright acid green and decorated with art by the members. It was a bar, but it was also a living museum, the succinct display of transgressing lives that bled into one another, drank into one another, became this one flamboyant thing. I knew about it vaguely, as the watering hole of artists like Francis Bacon and Damien Hirst, Lucian Freud, legendary people. But I had never quite imagined I would go there.

When we arrived, we went and sat in the corner; there were just a few other people there. The barman, chatting to an overweight man in his fifties with a stick and a glare. I looked out of another window, at more cobbled streets below – people who worked in the shops and bars chatting to each other in afternoon light, a woman carrying flowers with a solemn face. Tristan introduced me to the barman.

'She's an artist.' he said, which seemed embarrassing, not quite true. But the barman nodded unfazed.

'And how do you like your Bloody Mary?'

I looked around as I drank, at the acidic green walls. The rows and rows of bottles, the warmth and laughter and sarcasm, even early in the day. A home, of a kind. Kindred spirits, of sorts. That was the draw, at least. This sense of home, of coming home. This place to land, for a little while. Did I like him, or the Colony Rooms? Soho? One seemed an extension of the other, a guide to a world that would not be itself alone. Places and people merged and changed one another; characters could disappear into these spaces and become them, losing themselves in the most tender way. I did not think it but I felt it, the easy draw of fading into a place and becoming it. And Tristan was part of that place – this new transient home.

I sipped the Bloody Mary, but I didn't like it. Tristan told me about how Soho was changing for the worst.

'I loved the old Soho, the original Soho, but it's all on its way out. It's depressing,' he went on, 'the rents are just too high now. People keep moving away. Or dying. Don't know which is worse: Brighton or death? Seafront or Hell?' He shrugged. 'How's your drink?'

'Not bad at all. Thanks.'

More people began to fill the room, as the afternoon went on and we drank more. By the time the place was full of people, when those who were working had finished working, Tristan remembered he had some place to go.

'I have to meet someone,' he said, in a way that seemed regretful, tired. 'Almost forgot.'

'Who?' I asked. He smiled, looked down.

'You haven't really given up, have you?'

'I never really do,' he replied. 'That's why you should never, ever start.'

'Thanks for this afternoon,' I said.

'Stay in touch.'
'I will.'

He walked me to the tube. He hugged me goodbye and for a few moments I was elated, happy even. A new friend. A new situation excitingly dangerous and yet easy, sweet. The first person I had felt any connection to in months and months. Of all the people, him? But what did that matter – the stories, the reputation, the warnings. What did any of that really matter? I had known chaos as an enemy, but maybe now, if I let it, it could be my friend.

High and happy, until I stepped on the escalators and began to absorb the familiar claustrophobia, descending underground. Too many memories to avoid all the time, too many vulnerabilities, too many to count – nights back home I only wanted to blank out. I pushed through them with fantasies, deflections: part reality, mostly invention. Cocktails, experiments, magical things. Reality was negotiable; this is what I wanted to believe. This is what Tristan, by example, had already taught me.

When I got home, I ran a bath in my new flat mate's pink tub, with retro posters and pictures from magazines she had collaged onto the walls around it. There were a couple of dying houseplants by the small, frosted window above the toilet, half-finished bottles of toner and conditioner and face masks. I lay back and closed my eyes and tried to ignore the unfocussed urgency that now rose from the lethargy. It was as if I could see wounds being made on my anaesthetized skin but feel only a tiny scratch.

Disassociation, I had read, over and over again. The word didn't seem so bad. It seemed like a decision, like choosing not to associate with someone you don't like anymore. Like some casual detachment – not this physical thing, this struggling to fit together, to feel like a whole person, in any given moment. When did I feel whole? When someone looked at me and recognized something, saw me, somehow. A presumed and easy state.

I heard the doorbell ringing, a of couple new voices in the hallway. My flat mate Anya's friends, one familiar and one not. I lay in the bath a little longer and then, because it had become lukewarm, got out and went to my room. I could hear them laughing in the other room, drunk and content, and I felt inadequate. Anya always had people around her, was always talking and laughing. I still didn't know her that well; she was a friend of a friend who had a spare room.

Later, I went out for cigarettes and food from a corner shop. A limited choice, I settled on bread, pasta, eggs, wine, cigarettes. Sustenance, all coloured white and beige. Blue and white striped bag and a golden full moon. Commuters trickling back home wearily.

When I got back, Anya was playing Black Rebel Motorcycle Club talking to one of her friends, perched on a sofa, 'She's so weird, though,' someone was saying, and then they all went silent when I walked by. I smiled anyway, went into the kitchen, unpacked the beige foods. Boiled a kettle, put toast in the toaster, ignored the voices from the living room. Nervous laughter, or arrogant laughter? Both? I went into the living room with tea and toast, despite the awkwardness. It was cold because the window was open.

When they left, minutes later, I stayed in the living room for a bit, appreciating the silence. The fog of smoke slowly dissipated, and the record clicked to a stop. I boiled the kettle again and made another cup of tea, took it to my room. Silence was not silence, but an invitation, an emptiness aggressive in its desire to be filled. The voices, the people, the memories, returned in pointless, circular, waking dreams, so that they violated the present, too. When I'd finished the tea, I brushed my teeth, took a Xanax.

I let myself detach from those thoughts, the face, the body, the pain, or memory of pain – pain just once removed? – as the sedative trickled into my consciousness, dulling it gradually. To be nothing, to be asleep. To not get up in the morning. To not have to pretend, badly, that I was normal. Not weird. Not off. The pressure of it all. The pressure to not be weird. I was always going to disappoint, that was the thing.

In my lunch breaks, most days, I'd go and see him. It became routine, sitting on the red velvet window seat, smoking cigarettes as he chatted about his day. Who had dropped by who was making a film, who had insulted him. He sat at his desk and didn't seem to mind having me around. He was almost always wearing all black; I tended to match.

One Tuesday morning, I went along as usual; he was reading a magazine. 'A journalist has said I tried to kiss her,' he said, 'and she's made the entire interview about that.' He laughed. I shrugged, tapped some ash into a tray. My nonchalance, by now, was no longer a put-on. 'What do you think about that?' he asked.

'Did you not say anything interesting?' I replied. 'Was that why she felt the need to focus on that?'

He laughed again. 'Probably.'

I thought about kissing him then: was that what I wanted? Because that's where it was going.

I looked at him. Did I like him? Had I not from the beginning? Had I not, in a way, been planning this all along? Had I not, if I were honest with myself, given myself this role? Was he not the conquest, in a way? Yes, it was true, or I could tell myself it was true. I smiled at him, took another drag of another cigarette. Attention at any price. Some vague idea of being understood, needed, loved. Illusory, addictive things. But why had I set myself up like this? In a trap of my own making. I looked at the cigarette, also a stupid, addictive thing. Why did I smoke? Something to do. Something to pass the time as well, something disposable to hold.

He kissed me later that day, between cigarettes, just before I had to leave. Afternoon light, dust like tiny diamonds, flung slow motion in the air. Soft, kind, wrong. And then the power shifted,

I felt, and not to me. And yet I let it. Having the power, not having the power; they were both just ways to escape. To not be a person, but an action, a strategy, a pawn in my own, and his own, game. Romantic feeling became a weakness, a thing to overcome, or explore, in a way I thought was detached.

Power, powerlessness; I was intrigued. I wanted to know what it meant, I wanted to forget myself, too. I felt this stirring desire for a tender sort of revenge. I didn't know whether I was punishing this man, or myself. Intimacy could be, I knew so well, a weapon. Here, in this strange simulation, I had slightly more control over the damage than I did before. 'As long as we stay friends,' I said, as I left. 'That's the main thing.'

He smiled, imposed some energy over me as he did, and I realised I was weak. 'Of course,' he said.

A few weeks later we went to an exhibition opening. The exhibition was called 'Viva Lolita!' and it was supposed to be some kind of prank, us going together. I wore a pale pink baby doll dress, and he didn't change a thing. Black trousers, black sweater, black boots.

Fleetingly, beforehand, in his flat, he said that he was unsure about the prank: 'I'm not really that sort of person,' he said wistfully, as if he were the type of person to worry about his reputation.

'It's just a joke though,' I said. He looked down. 'Yes, I suppose it is.'

We went along, anyway, to a gallery about ten minutes from his flat. By the time we arrived, there were already people spilling out into the cobbled street with wine glasses, laughing in little, brightly coloured groups. We went inside, and he greeted one of the artists. He was wearing Adidas trousers, trainers, and a baggy, oversized T-shirt that said NO MORE FASHION VICTIMS.

'Why look at these paintings when I can look at her?' Tristan said to him, introducing me, in his way. 'She is Lolita.' I smiled, took a glass of white wine from a tray, and did not say a whole lot for myself. I was an art installation, after all.

I wandered around the gallery as he spoke to people, looking at the paintings. Were any of them really Lolitas? The only consistency was the colour scheme – murky pastels – and some nudity. Some generic, confused, nostalgic vision. I felt that I was underground, looking into an aquarium, at people who were not fully human. Mermaid-like creatures, barely-there things. Ghosts, clouds, sunken angels. Was this what men thought of girls, or was it what they thought of themselves? I positioned myself in front of one the paintings, a young figure wearing a lion mask, trying to imagine seeing it as they saw it, but I just felt very drunk. None of this had anything to do with people, it was just varying shades of consciousness, tepid waves of escapism, fragments of another world that was meant to be enticing but felt staid.

'Hey, come over here! Meet Stephen, he's one of the artists.'

I slipped back into my role without thinking about it. It was not the greatest stretch of the imagination, and yet it was still very much an act. I liked to think I was not really Lolita, that it was just a game.

'Hey,' I said. Safely in the cocoon of someone else's desires. 'Congratulations.'

The men laughed, and I did not think very much of them, but I didn't mind them either.

'You must be so proud,' I went on, sipped the rest of the wine.

'Maybe you can model for me one day?' Stephen asked.

'Maybe.' I shrugged. I looked as blank as I possibly could. 'Maybe, Stephen.'

꧁

We went out to dinner afterwards, to an Italian restaurant back in Soho, where Tristan had been going for years. Faded red tablecloths and paintings of little scenes somewhere in Italy. Small, chunky glasses, designed not to break, thick white napkins. We both ordered veal. I imagined a sad, innocent calf, and craved a cigarette instead, as the waiter delivered our meals. I drank more of the wine.

'How much have you had to drink already?' he asked, then.

'A glass or two?' I replied. 'There wasn't all that much to do at the opening. I thought that's what people did, anyway? I thought that was kind of the point of these things?' He smiled but he was annoyed, his eyes intensified with the mood, familiar now. I put the glass down.

'How's the veal?' He asked.

'It looks nice.'

He began eating. 'You should eat more. And drink less.'

'I don't do it intentionally.' I replied. 'I don't even drink that much. I'm just a lightweight.' I cut into the meat, though I was really not very hungry. Eating was an effort. I felt nervous to eat with him there.

'That's why you should eat more,' he went on. 'Everyone's a lightweight if they don't eat.'

'Are you?' He didn't answer me though. 'Why are you annoyed with me?' I asked. 'We didn't have to go to the exhibition.'

'You wanted to go,' he said.

'Just because you said we were going to go; *you* suggested it to begin with, so I thought we should go.'

He sighed. 'This is all becoming ridiculous.'

'Becoming?' He was angrier now though, and I felt some temptation just to irritate him further, to push it, to see the real him. The person behind this ongoing act.

'What's wrong?' I asked. 'Not what you paid for?'

'The veal's fine.' He replied. 'You should try it.'

He was tired, I could see that now. He wasn't just being moody for the sake of it. I started eating. The attention stirred some affection in me, even if I was only being told off. It meant he cared, in some way, I thought.

'I didn't mean to disappoint you,' I said, then. 'I tried to have a good time.' He placed his cutlery down.

'It's not that. It's not you,' he said. 'I'm sorry.' I wanted to help him, all of a sudden. Not to punish him anymore. Not annoy him. I wanted him to be happy.

'Can I come back to yours, tonight?' I asked.

'Of course. Of course, you can.'

We walked around after dinner; it was raining but neither of us had brought an umbrella. The puddles looked like pools of black ink or dark blood, tricking in between the cobble stones, glistening in the street lights. I only realised then, walking, that I was drunk, so absorbed by the little details, the things around me. People – Tristan – became vague impressions, no more present or significant than the streets or the buildings or the stars. All paper-thin, mismatched.

I liked his flat, now. It smelled familiar, of paint and cologne. He closed the shutters; I lit a cigarette. As he stood there, in profile, as I sat smoking, I realised how absorbed he was in himself, in his thoughts. And yet I couldn't stop watching, found him compelling, somehow.

※

It was a few weeks before I found out about his long-term girlfriend. It was an open relationship, apparently. I was not particularly phased in the beginning; I just shrugged, again. 'Okay,' I said. 'I guess that explains the other toothbrush in the bathroom, then.'

I was sitting in the window seat at the time, smoking again. He walked away, nodded. Nothing more was said. I looked towards his desk and noticed a photograph I must have seen before but somehow ignored: a woman in black and white. Full lips, glamorous, blonde. I stubbed out my cigarette, lit another.

He was in the kitchen, boiling a kettle. Why did I want him more, now? Standing there in the distance, ever so slightly less available than he had seemed five minutes ago.

During lunchtimes, I went to see him, though not as often. He was cooling off. Occasionally, I thought about just not going at all, of walking past his flat not going up to see him. Going somewhere else for lunch. Eating with one of my colleagues or eating alone. For a few days I would do this, but then I became more insecure again, unsettled and adrift in a city still strange to me. This spiralled into a generalised despair; it began to overwhelm my own efforts at control. Drinking, detaching, not eating enough; all these things began to work less and less. The chaos of emotion, which had seemed manageable before, began to spill over. Coping mechanisms switched sides; they were no longer helping me stay in control but tipping me further into chaos. I craved him more, then. A chat and a cup of tea, a hug. Somewhere to go, which didn't change. He had been this everyday escape and as he disappeared, the city closed in around me.

I went back again, and if I had been away for a few days, he was always relieved to see me. He would take me out, for drinks or to dinner. We talked about work, and his book. Other journalists, other girls. Sometimes, I told him how I felt, usually back in his flat, while smoking several cigarettes. That I felt out of place with my flat-mate and her friends, that I felt directionless, that I didn't fit together. He would nod and understand but with every conversation he also began to turn in on himself, some mood enveloping him, too, some boredom with me.

'What's wrong?' I said one day, over breakfast in an American style diner. It was old-school, lists of every variety of breakfast on a board above the counter, yellow and red bottles of sauce, filter coffee and the thinnest paper napkins. He was wearing black trousers and a ripped cashmere sweater again, eyes dark as the coffee, morose and attentive. His face was handsome and tired, his expression betraying a just held-together turmoil lived in too long.

'The launch again.' He replied. 'And me again. It never ends.' He tried and failed to smile. I knew what he was talking about, but I didn't want to push it. He brought it up anyway.

'I thought that you could save me from it, but you can't.'

'Save you from what?' He didn't want to say it. I didn't particularly want to hear it. I wanted him to say something else. It didn't seem glamorous or interesting to me anymore.

'It was a stupid thought, but I thought it anyway,' he went on. 'Exchange one intoxication for another. Idiotic.'

'It's a nice idea, but I'm no heroin.'

He laughed. 'And that's why I like you. But it's still a bad idea.'

'Your girlfriend?' He nodded, not looking me in the eye. 'Has she said something?'

'She'd like to meet you.'

I brushed it off. 'What would be the point in that?'

He smiled, unconvincingly. I finished my coffee.

How weird it was that I felt better when I was with him, even when everything was verging on chaos. When it was all about to fall apart, and it was clear to us both. Why did everything feel perfect, right then?

I didn't know why, and I didn't know why I felt it now, especially, but I did. Intimacy – was that it? Eating breakfast, the moment before everything was going to implode. There was something sweet about that. As if we were about to go into battle, knowing that we would not return together.

✼

Nobody set a date, but she appeared one Tuesday afternoon. She was wearing a white blouse and a figure-hugging black pencil skirt. Her hair was light blonde and wavy. She had crimson lips and a light tan. A couple inches shorter than me. I was already sitting in the large red chair, throne-like, when she came in, and at first she went to sit by the window. She drew it open, letting in a gust of wind and a cacophony of chatter, alarms and tinny music from the street below.

'That's better' she said, and then extended her hand to me, introducing herself.

'Hi.' I replied, and she sat down on the white shag carpet.

'I've just been shopping,' she said. 'Well, not really. My friend wanted to go shopping so I went with her. But she wanted to go to these glorified charity shops. But I just don't really get the whole vintage thing,' she went on. I wasn't sure if she was talking to me or Tristan. 'When other people go to charity shops, they find all these beautiful things. When I go, I just get reminded of old people.' She looked at me, and I smiled and nodded by default, as if in class. 'Apparently, though, we tend to like the clothes of whenever our parents were young. For me it's the seventies. I love seventies clothes.'

'My parents were different decades,' I replied. 'So maybe sixties and then eighties. But I'm not sure either one is for me.'

'Oh, I can see you in sixties clothes, though,' she said. 'Definitely. Like a little Jane Birkin or a Marianne Faithful? You'd suit those clothes.'

'Thanks.'

Tristan did not interrupt this conversation; he busied himself with something that involved lots of papers and magazines. He was looking for something, apparently. I kept smoking. She lit up a menthol.

'Are they healthier then? More than regular cigarettes?'

She shrugged. 'Maybe. I just like the taste.' The smoke faded around her powdered face, into her hair; she breathed in, and out. Picked something from her nail. I looked over at Tristan, who was still supposedly looking for something on his desk, nervously.

'I should smoke less,' I said. 'I don't even really like smoking all that much. I just do it out of boredom.'

'Do you get bored a lot, then?'

'Not these days,' I said. She smiled, then.

She turned to Tristan. 'Oh, did you hear about Mark?' She asked him. 'Mark's an old friend of ours, sort of,' she said to me briefly. 'He died,' she said to Tristan. 'Hanged himself.'

'I heard,' he replied. Maybe that was why he seemed depressed, I thought. He was always going on about death, but in moments he seemed genuinely haunted by the prospect. It seemed to drip from him, sometimes, like sticky black ink, pulling him to the ground in a puddle. And part of him, it became clear, was addicted to that. The sickly-sweet pit, the melting of his worries, the aching into oblivion. He yearned for it as he feared it, or yearned for peace, anyway.

'In the Highlands.' she went on. I imagined that, without wanting to. A tree somewhere remote. All alone. 'I can think of better ways to go, myself.' she went on.

'Like what?' I asked.

'Well, something not too painful, ideally.' She went on, arching her back and looked into the distance, comfortable there. Her bare feet nestled in the cream shag rug like pearlescent eggs. 'An overdose, maybe.' she said. 'That's how old people go, isn't it? 'She died in her sleep', they say.' She rolled her eyes, as if all this was very futile. 'But it's not the worst way to go. How would you?' She looked at me pointedly as she said this, with her bright, teasing eyes.

'Oh, probably the same.' I replied. 'Drowning sounds romantic but apparently it's very painful.' She nodded, agreed, with a superficial morbidity.

'How would you go?' She asked Tristan, then. He smiled sadly. Brown eyes, melancholic like a clown dressed in white, the tight rope a step away.

'You know me,' he said flatly. 'Death by speedball.'

'Do you really love her, then?' I asked the next afternoon, lying in his bed. Crisp white sheets, cigarettes, faraway sirens through the window.

'I do,' he said.

'Do you love me too?'

'I do.' He looked depressed about it, though. That was the problem. I didn't have anything else to say, any way to make whatever it was better. Any other place to go.

'She thinks you're crazy, you know.'

'Maybe I am, to be involved in all this.'

'Almost certainly,' he said. He didn't say anything but there was a moment when I realised I didn't have to be involved. I didn't have to stay. I didn't have to see his girlfriend again. I could just leave and go elsewhere and see other people. But I wanted to, I understood then. I really didn't want to go. And as I realised this, I knew that I was on my way out.

Not now, not even next week, but at some point. I was a fleeting thing, impermanent, disposable. Hair and lips and skin. He cared about me, but he was someone who disposed of himself regularly enough; I would be no different. I knew that. 'I should probably go soon,' I said, then, and he nodded. I got dressed and picked up my bag to leave.

'Come back whenever you want,' he said, though I was not sure that he really meant it. I looked at him before I left; he was tired, pale, weak. As I walked back to work, I thought about the investment of it: he'd been doing heroin for about as long as I had been alive, the stretch of my life to date. It was like bringing up a child, this addiction. And for a moment he had thought that maybe another child could make up for this deathly one, exorcise this ghost who wouldn't leave. But he could not be saved, and perhaps we both knew that all along. We were replaying stories of slow, lingering deaths, and repressed grief, and lost youths. Reliving things through one another, vampires in a dragging waltz.

Later that night, I couldn't sleep. I watched the glare of the street light through the edges of the curtains, the flickering lights of passing cars and vans. I heard the foxes and late-night pedestrians screeching and stomping around. I checked my phone a hundred times, listened to music and then listened to the silence, for the low hum of electrical things, the faintest murmurs of my flat-mate next door.

Usually, if I couldn't sleep, I would take a sleeping pill, but I was running low, and wanted to wean myself off, to try at least. They had stopped working so well anyway. But I couldn't sleep. Couldn't switch off. I just let myself think, remember, regret. This affair, friendship, thing, had given me a purpose, and now it was slipping away. Short run of a play. Replacement actress. Or had I only ever been an understudy? No, I had my own part, but it was a fleeting one, a stock character. I stayed awake until dawn, had to call in sick. I took a pill in the end, which swiped my angst in a single blow.

As the weeks went on, I did everything possible to blank out everything and everyone, except the music, and the dry green grass, and those others sharing their bright despair, casually. I kept dancing to forget – shunning the lonely, crashing moments, those memories that seeped back into consciousness in the early morning or as I walked down empty streets. I kept trying to forget but couldn't help thinking about it every day, every hour, in between the songs and new people.

They followed me everywhere, these bullets of memory skimming around my head. Lists of distant cities on airline websites. Dreams of other places, of starting over and then leaving again. Punctuating life with destinations, mental and physical. Levels of altitude and drunkenness, cities and substances yet untried. Days and weeks to whittle away. Spraying perfume and opening windows, taking baths together and cutting each other's hair. Dirty sheets and torn clothes, soft wet skin, dark hair. Visions in the morning. I went swimming, the water glittering more than usual; fire in my bloodstream, chlorine in my hair, tiny people looking down from the balcony. It's funny, anyway, I thought to myself. The whole thing is funny, I'll give it that.

I got kicked out of my room the next month, couldn't go back to work anymore. I couldn't afford to stay to London at all. I wanted to make good choices, sometimes, but instead I chose alcohol and little parcels of powder, I chose putting myself behind a wall that nobody could ever penetrate, my own fortress. I chose stimulations, patterns, habits. Obsession for the sake of it. I read Nietzsche, highlighted, 'It is not the desired that we love, but the desire itself.' I desired desire because it was something to hide behind. It was attention, unwavering. Attention that never saw me; I would not be left alone.

Tristan had emailed me from time to time, and I saw him once or twice, over the course of my first and second years at university. He was good at making me think that I didn't belong anywhere else but with him. I started avoiding him, though. When an old mutual friend got in touch, one sunny morning in June, we had not spoken in a few months. I hadn't been expecting a call, but I picked up anyway.

'It's Tristan.' he said, immediately. 'He's dead. I just had to say it – I'm sorry. I know you've had your ups and downs. Crack and heroin. This morning.'

After exchanging commiserations, we hung up, and then I looked at my friend, who had been standing with me. 'Tristan died,' I said, 'of an overdose.'

Then I looked around at the perfect garden, blooming and easy and serene with the light. I was angry with him – that he had died when everything was so beautiful. 'How could he do this?' I asked, to no one in particular.

'I'll get you a drink,' she replied, and for a moment I was left standing there, dumbstruck and alone.

※

We drifted through the rest of that afternoon. We lay out in a park for a few hours, and I got sunburnt. Later, we went to a party together and saw all our other friends. We stood together on the edge of the crowd, in someone's basement kitchen, with people spilling outside into a small garden. All the girls were wearing maxi dresses and sunglasses, the boys in jeans and shorts.

Another friend came over at one point: 'I just heard,' he said. 'I'm so sorry. How are you feeling about it all?'

'I just can't take it in right now,' I said, and I drank some more wine, very slowly. 'It's just hard to believe.'

He nodded. 'I can imagine,' he said, but could he? I wouldn't have imagined it this way, so vague and disarming. I imagined Tristan's face, but I pushed it away. I was angry, still. Even if he hadn't meant it. Especially if he hadn't meant it. And I missed him, like I always had, and more than I ever had, even as I was repelled. I had been placed into a story I didn't want to be in, and now I was sucked in further, unable to push away emotions that only confused me. I wanted none of it.

The funeral was two weeks later, after an autopsy. It was, as his friend had said that first afternoon, an overdose. 'Death by speedball,' as he had once predicted himself. But it had not been suicide, apparently; the coroner had ruled a death by misadventure. And yet what was long-term drug abuse, other than a drawn-out suicide?

Perhaps it was not that at all, though. What did I know? I felt immediately so weary and so small, so unprepared. None of it really made sense; or perhaps, it was just too obvious, too unfulfilling because it was so obvious. It seemed so predictable and yet such a waste. The answer and the end had been there all along. Of course, he would die – of course the man who thought about dying all day, who wavered between affairs and heroin, would die on a beautiful summer's day, way too soon.

At the funeral I sat with my editor, who had warned me off him in the beginning. We sat in a pew of St. Patrick's surrounded by all of Soho dressed brash and overtly seductive, like he'd have wanted. I was twenty-one by then. I wore a black lace dress I had bought in Berlin that Spring. I had dyed my hair back to brown.

I'd last seen him only a few months previously. He seemed to be good spirits then, but he had taken me along to witness him signing his Will. The lawyer seemed to think it was slightly odd, but, as with everything back then, I just took it in my stride, because I no longer knew what was weird and what was not. I had no sense of perspective or convention. But this was weird. His dying was weird. I was relieved that we had made up in the end. And yet something about that whole period seemed to cling to me, creep on me, no matter what efforts I made to move on.

The whole thing was messed up really. He was in his early forties when we met. It was obvious enough he was using early on, but I was naïve, and it was not exactly my place to judge or even worry. 'Don't ever start,' was all he said. And later: 'I've been intoxicated by you since I met you. I thought you could replace it, that was a stupid idea. You can't save a rat like me.'

And yet for years, something in what he said and did must have stayed with me, because he was not the last. I found new versions of him, men who longed for salvation in some other person, who was looking for the same thing, and failing badly.

※

The Wake unravelled over twelve hours in a nearby members' club. Towards the end, I noticed a man sitting in a very large armchair, and he smiled at me, beckoned me over. I wasn't sure if we had met before; he seemed familiar in some way, but I couldn't place him. But then, I figured, there were many nights I didn't fully remember.

'Have we met?' I asked him.

'I don't think so,' he replied. 'I'm Nate. You were Tristan's friend, weren't you?'

'That's right,' I replied.

'So was I,' he went on. 'This is the last place I ever saw him alive. Sitting in this chair.' It was a large armchair, and he moved along to make space for me. 'There's room for you too, if you want?' I was so tired by the Wake, by this point, that I went and sat with him there and we talked about our memories of Tristan, the nicer memories, as the Wake went on around us. I was beginning to feel too much a part of whatever this was, this ghoulish place – far too much at home, in this morbid, sprawling family.

I wavered between detachment and intimacy so frequently, and that, I realised, was what made it feel so close to home. And yet, with all this velvet and insanity, with everything good and bad about Soho in a single room and a single event, I felt uneasy. What had I been looking for in Tristan? It only occurred to me years later to ask myself that.

Perhaps, again, it was too obvious. I was looking for someone older, to give me attention, to show me around. A friend. A way to meet people, and someone to protect me, too. Someone to talk to, all day, about everything. And he was all of those things, and he was kind sometimes. But it was also lopsided and damaging. I was his Lolita; he had said it himself. I wanted to be someone else, and in a way my wish was granted. I wanted to disappear, like he did, and in moments we were successful.

But I could not, a decade later, still repeating myself in strange ways, downplay the destruction as much as I had then. Escapism was not light-hearted and frivolous; he had died, after all and I had spent the next decade in a cycle of depression and intense infatuations, replaying the first disastrous one. What was I looking for? What was I still looking for? Even as I was aware of the consequences this relationship had, I struggled to move on from it, repeating history in the sorts of men I chose to be with, the underworld that I could never quite leave. This inability to move on frustrated me endlessly; faces lingered as I tried to sleep.

In the months immediately after his death, I moved around, and then the months bled into years, and the ink bled into the paper, and at art school I made repetitions of repetitions, photographing and printing out faces and memories until they had transformed into something else, merely a figment of my imagination. That was the greatest dream, that it was all a fiction, that it had never really happened at all.

Those years were a confusion, a half-hearted attempt to stay alive, to kill time, and also to preserve time. I kept on working, I applied for more academic courses and scholarships and grants when my degree ended, because I could still not face the real world. I ended up on a PhD course in photography, in which I could lose myself in other people's perspectives, lives, and objects – deconstructing them for a few academics, and then teaching students not much younger than myself.

'A photograph captures a little time,' I would say to them, 'the longer the shutter is open, the more time is captured – and so you can focus on what has already gone, you can preserve something passed.' I told them about Susan Sontag and Nan Goldin. I dwelled, too, in this nether land of nostalgia and lost things. 'All photography is memento mori,' Sontag wrote. We studied death, abstracted and desired; we staved it off. I lived in this graveyard of icons and lost things, willing them to stay, refusing to leave them entirely.

※

After the funeral, I stayed in touch with Nate, feeling bonded on account of this shared and strange bereavement. We met on the Heath, later that summer, and as soon as I saw him again, I felt a wave of liberation, a profound joy, that finally he was here. That from all the unhappiness of Tristan's death, he had emerged, and we could be friends. We drank rum that afternoon and went swimming in the ponds; the water seemed green and cloudy as absinthe. Whilst others panicked about river-borne diseases that summer, I had never been happier.

In the months that followed, he would always show up in a magical way, whenever I was having a bad time. Whether I was at a party or in my room, he would just appear, and I would lighten, and that same sense of freedom would return. And yet he was escaping things too, and battling things too, and came in and out of my life, never staying in one place for very long. I thought I was chasing freedom and yet men became my weakness, with our shared desire for escape strangely smothering. I fetishized surrender and servility, a particular kind of friendship, a deep co-dependency. I still wanted to be saved. And though I never articulated it as such, I wanted to save them too. I longed for escape, but I did not realize that I would have to give this freedom to myself, that I would have to give myself permission, rather than long to be given it by other people.

At times, though I thought I craved freedom, really I sought out guidance and structure from other people, the reassurance of being told what to do. I sought a fresh version of a dynamic that had once stifled me; I sought intimacy in too-closeness, a play at rebellion that always taunted me with the reality of being trapped again.

When this began to happen, as it quickly did – when feeling stuck became the defining feature of every pursuit, via a relationship, to be free – I indulged the misery with songs and stories. I'm not sure why I felt I needed the voice of a singer or a fictional character to feel my own emotions, but I always did, and in their songs and stories, in hearing my own pain vicariously, I found one sort of freedom: the space to feel something, even something that hurt.

These relationships, their ups and downs, gave me a way out of numbness, where before I had grown up believing I could not voice any complaint, that it would be an inconvenience, a personal slight against my parents. But first in music and books, and then in the relationships, I waded into a world of emotion that I had felt cut off from before. And though it was overwhelming, I had been craving this expanse for many years.

With other people I found a form of escapism I was committed to. This pursuit of love felt like religious practice; divine and human love seemed to become ever more entwined and confused as the years went on. Love could be a form of mysticism, in this desire for a mutual transcendence from the worst of life, or even just the most mundane. I had this unending faith that love could conquer all, every wound and slight, every pit of sadness; it could counter every unfathomable loss, the existential crisis at our hearts. It was a losing game, a kaleidoscopic glimpse of ourselves in people who would leave us.

4

WHEN WE FIRST approached the island in our boat, I had glimpsed a row of cottages by a steep cliff, and it turned out that this is where we would be staying. After a short hike, where we were followed by gulls at first, who grew disinterested the further we walked, I could see the row of cottages again, the other side of a steep hill. There were signs of life on the way, some old bottles collected in a crate, a battered kayak leaning against a wall, but no people that I could see anywhere. I asked him where I would be sleeping.

'You'll be in my cottage,' Nate replied, as he led the way up one more path, with a grassy expanse either side of us, seeming strangely vulnerable under the stone-grey sky, as if it might drop down and crush us at any moment. 'The others are in the other two, but people do move around, and we all meet for most meals. There are the various classes and activities, too, but I have quite a lot of other work to do.'

'I won't interrupt you,' I said, in case he was worried about that.

'It's okay;' he smiled warmly again, as he helped me over a ditch, 'I have a separate studio. And you'll have other work too. There is always more work to do, always things falling apart. And then there is the cooking. We try to make sure there is not too much time for distraction; it's better for everyone that way.'

As we climbed further up the path, there were so many birds around us, but they seemed not to mind us there and they were not squawking so much anymore; they just stared at us and then flew away if we walked too close to them. The waves crashed against their cries in a lazy rhythm and already I felt acclimatised to them.

'And what about the researchers, you mentioned helping them?' I had not seen any so far, though I realised now that they had probably been the other people on the boat; they had been so quiet and withdrawn we had not spoken at all.

'Only if they ask us to.' Nate replied. 'Or if we see anything unusual, we just have to report it to them. Like a whale or something. But I'll show you the things to look out for when we get to the cottage. You just need to keep your eyes open, that's all.'

I was impressed by how organised Nate was now; when we had first met, in our early twenties, he had been anarchic and delirious, floating from one thing to another in an ethereal way, but now he had grounded himself in this utopian regime. On the island, especially, he seemed calmer than ever; his smile conveyed a new warmth to me. It was as if the landscape was so wild and beautiful that he no longer had to try so hard to find those qualities in himself; he merely turned his attention to all this and became peaceful.

When we arrived closer to the row of cottages, I still couldn't see anyone else, and it was beginning to rain. There were three buildings altogether, around a patch of cobbled stones that made up a little street, built nearly two hundred years ago according to Nate.

'They'll be working or meditating,' he explained, when I asked him where the others were, and he opened the door to his cottage. 'You can stay here.' He signalled to a single bed draped with several blankets and a thick duvet, the other side of the room. 'And I'm in the back room, if you need me.'

The space was otherwise open plan, with a small kitchen and an open fireplace. It was rudimentary but welcoming, and Nate had some of his paintings and other artworks on the walls. A portrait caught my eye – a woman lying on a bed. He noticed me looking at it and said, 'that's by Hana; you'll meet her later too.'

After I had unpacked my things, we left the cottage again, so he could show me around. 'A long time ago, this was a monastery, with a little Abbey.' he said, pointing at some ruins in the distance.

'There were many pilgrimages over the centuries, until the Vikings came from Denmark and destroyed everything. Then they were here only briefly, and it was deserted until the 1800s, when a tiny village was built – and that's why we have these cottages, and some cobble stones in the street, and the harbour. But they died out, and it has been mostly uninhabited ever since. Researchers have been looking after it mostly, but we're the first to come here for any reason other than the birds. We have to be very careful. We only have permission because we're helping with the research, and because we're helping preserve the history. That's what I've been working on, partly – an artistic response to the history, especially the pilgrimages. And the Priest, you'll meet him in a moment, he's here to help with that.' We walked on until we were closer to the ruins, where the Priest, who was the same age as us, and who I wasn't completely sure was really a Priest, was sitting.

'Finally!' he said as he saw us, going up to Nate and hugging him, before shaking my hand. 'I was beginning to wonder if the boat had been cancelled again.'

'No, but we had to leave our things at the cottage first, sorry about that. This is Lena, anyway. She can help us with the project.'

I smiled along with this, though I had not realised that my contribution was to be so specific. The Priest smiled; he was wearing a waterproof black coat with a hood, and he seemed cheerful, shaking my hand. He had the darkest blue eyes and black hair cut short, and he seemed at one with the place.

'This is where we have some of our ceremonies, Lena,' Nate went on. 'Although the abbey was destroyed almost a millennia ago, we have resurrected their rituals in the ruins. It's our way of preserving history.'

'It's also what we told the Arts Council we would do,' the Priest explained dryly. 'And I have informal meetings here too, with whoever needs to talk.' He looked at me to suggest that that might be me, too, though I just kept smiling. It was beginning to feel more and more like an Arts Council funded cult, though I tried to remain open-minded.

'Are you a Catholic priest then, or?'

Nate laughed as I said this, and the Priest smiled. 'Sorry, I should have clarified. He's not ordained; he's a theology PhD. He's researching pilgrimages, and this one in particular,' he said blithely. 'But I'm sure he can help with any crises of faith if you need that.'

'I was thinking, before coming here, that maybe I do need an exorcism,' I said. The Priest laughed then. 'Perhaps I have a spiritual problem, not a mental health one.'

He smiled. 'And have you thought about praying, Lena?'

'I do sometimes. But so far, I'm not sure it's really working. I think I need a miracle.'

'This island is a miracle, Lena. You are in the right place now.' I wasn't sure if he was being serious, and I was not even sure if I was being serious anymore, but when he said this, he seemed earnest, the way Nate always was whenever he talked about the island. Their love of the place, regardless of what spiritual or creative concerns led them here, was quite infectious; despite feeling disarmed by the set-up, on some level, I did not want to leave.

Nate and I walked back to the cottage after that, where he said everyone would be meeting that evening for dinner. 'I have some work to do first, so just make yourself at home.' I was relieved he said that, because I was suddenly quite exhausted from the traveling and sea air. I took the opportunity to nap, resting underneath a blue woollen blanket on my new bed. Though it was scratchy,

I nestled into it, wrapping myself around it in a foetal position, the distant noise of the waves hitting the cliffs lulling me softly to sleep.

When I awoke – I'd fallen into a deeper sleep than I had meant – the cottage was filled with a few other people, including the Priest from before and a man in a Hawaiian shirt with bleach blonde hair. Nate had lit citronella candles that gave off a sweet citrus and vanilla scent, and a few people were sitting cross-legged on the floor as he lounged on the sofa. There was a plate of oysters on the low table, and tea lights in shallow green tumblers.

'There she is!' he said, as I opened the door. He had lit a fire, which cast glowing shapes on the rough stone walls. 'This is Lena, everyone. She's joining us here for a while.'

'Hi Lena,' they said in unison. For a moment I felt as though Nate might have tricked me; this seemed like what I imagined an AA meeting to be like, which I had been intentionally avoiding. But when they all introduced themselves, they did not say they were alcoholics. In fact, no one mentioned anything of the sort; as I sat at the foot of a large maroon armchair, they discussed what they were cooking later in the week, as they helped themselves to the fresh oysters, and when there would be a delivery to the harbour, and what the researchers had said when they met earlier. Still sleepy, most of it went over my head, and for the first time in many months, I allowed myself to relax, and give in to the warm atmosphere, the ease of this group, who seemed to welcome me so readily as one of their own. Finally, I found myself thinking. I am at home.

I still woke several times in the night for those first few days, without any sleeping pills to rely on, but Nate was very congratulatory about my new sobriety. And yet the lack of sleep began to disturb me; in my dreams, I couldn't stop ruminating on the beginning of my relationship with Aidan. The ease with which I settled here now, to this rock in the North Sea, allowed me the freedom to remember everything that had led me here more fully. I started unwinding, and as I did so my memories clarified, though I tried to remain otherwise detached, unafflicted by nostalgia, which had kept me prisoner for so long.

5

GLASGOW, 2020

I HAD FIRST met Aidan in Glasgow five years earlier, through Nate. He had been living there for four months, having moved in with his friend Danny, who had already been living there a few years. I was in London at that point, where I was mostly teaching in a casual, draining way, following my PhD; I was getting fed up, though, despite my efforts.

'Are you back in Glasgow?' I had messaged Nate sometime in January of that year, wanting to see him. 'Got an exhibition I need to review there soonish so could meet up if you wanted?'

'Back early next month wld that work?'

'Maybe end of the month? Need to get out of London.'

'That wld wrk 4 me / lingered too long there myself.'

Eventually we met up. Nate greeted me with a warm smile and a big hug. It was freezing outside, and we met at an Art Deco bar and restaurant that specialised in lobster and oysters and champagne and other things we couldn't afford. We ordered Guinness and sandwiches instead.

'How are you finding Glasgow then?' I asked. Nate lounged back, sipping his coffee slowly. He had a pencil thin moustache that I wasn't sure about. His hair was very neat. He had brought a book with him, but I couldn't see the title.

'Good, good, very fresh air,' he said. 'I've been going to the outdoor gym, trying to stay fit.' I wasn't sure if he was joking; he seemed serious.

'Isn't it a little cold for that?'

'No, it's great, because nobody else is there!'

I wondered what he was really doing in Glasgow, but I didn't ask. A few years ago, he had been in art school as well, but I didn't know what else he had been doing since then, and he was not particularly forthcoming.

'I haven't been here in ages,' I said. 'I can't even remember the last time.'

'You should come over more then.' He said this so matter-of-factly but so finally, his brown eyes locking mine, as if he were ringing a bell that would summon me.

'I want to.' I replied. 'I can't deal with London anymore. There's nothing to do there anymore, no one to see. Teaching takes up so much time even though it's only part-time . . .' I rambled on. '. . . and I know that there are things going for London, I know that. I have a special place in my heart for it, I really do, but it's a relief to be out. I've been there too long now.'

He nodded patiently, drank his coffee. 'Mmmm. You should just come to Glasgow then.'

'I keep meaning to. I need a break from it all. I need a reset.'

'We should do meditation then,' he went on, more excitedly now that he was pulling me in again. 'We should do Pilates. Yoga. I've been meaning to for a while now actually. I need to be healthy. I need a new life!'

'Okay,' I agreed. 'We can have a new life.'

He started looking up classes on his phone. 'Here, there's one on Monday mornings, 10 a.m.' I didn't realise he was being so serious and in such an immediate way, but I went along with his idea.

'Sure, sounds potentially doable . . .' We were surrounded by quite elderly people, dressed up for their martini lunches, and the old-fashioned waiters. There was the feeling of being on a cruise, as if we had just decided to retire at twenty-seven and join them all early. Had we retired from life? Almost. This was a much-needed hiatus, a moment of recovery, he said. Emotional burn-out? Failure? No, just a much-needed break. Something like that, anyway. He gave me a sarcastic look, which would in time become very familiar to me.

I tried to think that I was at least free now, and I might even have found a new city, potentially. But I wasn't sure, for all Nate's enthusiasm, that moving again could achieve much. Ever since Tristan had died, I had chased a restlessness that I couldn't shake, and which emerged wherever I went and whatever I did. I was still here, in my head, enveloped by some mood, in a steady disappearance from the world.

I thought of Tristan again, how I had found in him a decadent, chaotic father figure, drawn to him only for him to die as my father had, from another sort of illness. And ever since, I had been attending to and mourning similar men; revisiting romantic dissolution with each infatuation, turning enchantment into a monotonous reality. Only I could ruin every intense romance, turn light and fun to misery.

'Perhaps Glasgow does make sense,' I said, regardless, as if the answer to all this was just to charge ahead anyway.

'It always makes sense.' Nate said. 'Here,' as our food arrived, salt beef sandwiches. 'These are the best.' I was starving, had until very recently been entirely off my food. I had been mostly vegan for the past year, but I gave in to this new hunger.

'Not bad,' Nate said, biting into it, as I did too, the horseradish stinging my tongue.

Later, when it was already dark, we went to an exhibition opening. I wasn't reviewing this one; we were just going for the free drinks. But it turned out to be good. It was a group show; I became transfixed by these ethereal, larger than life figures painted onto some of the walls, as if dancing – wrapping their limbs around each other, merging into one another, becoming one entity. They were dancing in the walls, cut off from the visitors but also one and the same, and extension of the crowd – this parallel world of the night-time, the dreams we had. A shared, familiar, lulling fantasy.

We wandered around. Nate was wearing a long, vampish coat, his hair slicked back, managing to appear both intense and languorous, mocking and sweet. We didn't take very long to see everything else there was to see and then leave.

After that, we went to another gallery, showing some abstract art this time – large canvases in single pastel colours, nothing more. The atmosphere and the work were not especially amenable, either. Inside: a crowd of cut-off jeans and converse, oversized trucker jackets, hair cut roughly by hand (or intended to look that way), and turned up beanie hats, sitting an inch above their ears. We headed for the drinks table, avoiding the roaming, judging eyes, swerving through little crowds of people who were so determined only to speak to one another, and yet to be seen doing so. We took the free bottles of beers and giggled to each other like teenagers, pretending to be more engaged with the work than we were, moving around in circles.

We walked outside into the night, after one more circuit, into the harsh, biting cold, wrapping scarves around our faces, walking up towards the station, shivering. Past all the restaurants and bars full of couples and steamed up windows. Old men smoking outside the bars and restaurants, facing out to the street even as they talked to each other.

※

One evening, a few days later, Nate suggested another evening out. Just a small, local thing, he said, in the bar around the corner from his apartment. We went there around eight, to this old Edwardian pub, and I ordered a Guinness. The bar was old fashioned, with crimson velvet seats, dark wood tables and black and white tiled floors, and a partition between two rooms.

Moments after we sat down with our drinks, a man walked in, and he seemed to know Nate. He looked over at me, then, and we both smiled immediately, though we had never met. The man disappeared and returned with drinks, and then sat directly across from me on the wine-red seat. He seemed drunk, faded, and I was too. I was also intoxicated by him already, and I smiled again.

'I'm Aiden, by the way,' he said. A scar on his lip, the exact same scar as mine. What were the chances? He was a photographer as well, he said, as he looked at me, sat closer still. He had been living in Glasgow a couple years, about ten minutes from Nate. He had been at Glasgow School of Art before that, had grown up on Skye.

'I wish I lived here,' I said, and he moved closer again. He noticed we drank the same drink.

'I can't drink anything else,' I replied, which was not entirely true. I just couldn't drink any other beer. I was lost in his eyes and would say anything to keep him looking back; he was doing the same.

Nate and his other friends began to move away, after a few minutes of this, and I joined Aidan, sitting beside him. He touched my leg, moments later.

'I wish I could kiss you,' he said after that. I wanted to kiss him too. He had the most perfect lips, I thought. Impossibly handsome. I could not look away or even move slightly apart from him; I was, just like that, completely enchanted. A single hoop in one ear, deep brown eyes, at least in this light. He was dark and familiar; his eyes stayed with me, hooked me in. And I was hooking him in too, too. The same scar as me, the same scar on his lip. It seemed romantic, fateful even; as we talked more, even our problems were strangely aligned. The main problem, of course, was that we had not slept together yet. This seemed, already, some kind of travesty.

We told each other our stories as the evening went on, which overlapped in the dark places; the ghosts of our dead fathers, a shady Underworld of lost things. He touched my leg again; we ordered more drinks, sat inches, then less, apart. He could drown in my eyes, he said. I was drowning in his.

I was captured, and happily so. I forgot all my problems in the moments I was his, which began, somehow, immediately. I forgot that this was the problem, the problem I had and would not let go – this wanting to be someone else's, this wanting to be consumed. This wanting submission. This wanting to see it reflected in the mirror of someone else's eyes. This like for like; for an eternity expanding in an evening. That was the dream I could never quite relinquish. These nights, I was sure, were the best part of life itself; I would never give them up, I would always dive in.

He walked me home that night and kissed me on the doorstep and said he would be in touch. He texted soon after, before I'd gone to sleep. Let's do dinner, he said. Soon, he said. He knew a nice place, he said, had been meaning to go.

I slept until eight the next morning, awoken by the light. I lay there a little longer, aware that no one else was up yet. The sun streamed into the room, and I listened to some music, wondering why I didn't have a hangover, despite all the Guinness. After staying there for a while longer, I went to the kitchen for a glass of water. Nate's flat mate Danny was up now, boiling the kettle, bright, blue eyes sparkling. The morning sun glowed in every surface. I could never be in a bad mood around Danny. He made tea and then I made some coffee, and we sat together at a long dark dining table in the kitchen. Nate emerged soon after.

'He's actually been awake for hours,' Danny said wryly, 'but he only gets out of bed as soon as he hears the kettle boil, when he knows someone else is already making breakfast.'

Danny went to the shop while we sat in the kitchen drinking coffee. Nate yawned and chopped up red onions and put English muffins and bacon under the grill, dropping eggs into vinegary boiling water.

'We're thinking of going to this flea market thing at some point later this morning,' he said. 'You can come if you want to.'

'Sure. I just have to do some work in the afternoon. I have some essays to finish marking before the deadline tomorrow.'

'How many?'

'Altogether? About sixty.'

'That's intense.'

'If I wanted to do this all the time, I would have done teacher training, not a PhD. And it's not as if anyone is really hiring anyway . . .'

Nate turned back to the grill. 'You should just move here then,' he said, again, as if it were easy to just up and leave. But maybe it was? I had moved house every year since I was nineteen. What was one more move?

'I'd have to wait until June,' I replied. 'I'd have to find a flat . . . Get more freelance work . . . or even an actual job.'

'You'll be fine,' he said. 'There are summer school jobs, babysitting, that sort of thing.'

'Aidan said that as well.' Nate looked up at me with a questioning look, not entirely approving, when I said this.

'How was last night, then?' he asked pointedly, as if he were my father. 'I was relieved you came back in one piece.'

'Oh, it was nice, thanks. I really like him. It was kind of intense though, I can't really explain it.' Nate stood up tensely and checked the grill again, then started washing out the coffee pot.

'He is an intense guy,' he replied, 'from what people say,' and he looked me in the eye quite sternly, then put the pot down. 'I'm not one to warn people off other people, it's not something I really agree with, as a rule. But in this case, I would make an exception. Maybe I should have said before you went out with him, or before you even met him – but as soon as I saw you both together the other night, my heart sank.'

He sat down as he said it; I had rarely seen him so serious. 'Aiden can be very charming, but he is a compulsive liar; he uses people. He uses women, especially. He has been like this for years. And he just keeps getting away with it! Probably because he is good looking, or just extremely determined.' He rolled his eyes at this, then went on. 'He reels people in. And then he turns on them. By all means, be friends with him, if you really want, but please don't let it go beyond that. You would *not* be a good match.' But as he said all these bad things, my heart quickened, the dreaminess returned.

'I liked him though, Nate.' I replied. 'There was such a connection . . . We just talked and talked,' but I was failing to communicate it to him, apparently, as he remained disapproving. 'I just can't explain it.' I was surprised by my own intensity, now, but he just rolled his eyes.

'I can't keep you,' he said, and then he turned around back to the grill and took out the muffins and bacon, put them on a plate, followed by the eggs, which he had poached. 'Here you go,' he said, and then we both ate, and said nothing more about Aidan that morning.

Outside, it began to rain heavily, so that the pavements darkened several shades, and Nate shut the window, steam gathering into drops our side of the glass instead. He wiped up the golden yolk with his toast, smearing it over the plate like a stroke of paint.

Later, we made snacks and tea and then lounged around in the kitchen for a while before lounging around in the living room for a change of scene. I started reading a book on the photography of Francesca Woodman as Nate read The Pursuit of Love by Nancy Mitford. He was lying down on the sofa, wrapped up in a pink blanket. I was sitting on the other sofa, with another cup of coffee. Gulls swooped by in the street, chasing after discarded chips, eyes on careless children, seeming to lay heavy on the breeze.

'How long do you think you'll stay in Glasgow?' I asked him. I had wondered because he kept suggesting I move, but he had never said if he intended to stay.

'We'll see,' he said. 'I get bored if I do anything beyond one year, generally. This is the longest I've ever lived anywhere. Usually, I don't last more than six months. I'm onto month seven, here . . .'

'You are staying though, aren't you?'

He smiled, shrugged. 'Maybe,' he said.

'You have to stay,' I said. 'Because I want to move here now. So you can't just leave as soon as I finally get here.'

'I'm not going anywhere just yet.'

We went back to our books.

※

Aidan messaged me before we met again, telling me about the project he was working on. He had a show coming up and he was creating an elaborate set for some photographs, with slow-moving silver liquids, captured at a slow shutter speed, so it would be moving in two dimensions at once, in two forms. The real and the representation would flow both ways, he said. Abstract shapes would emerge naturally from a strange liquid; it would be a thing of sublime beauty, a silver wave, a shining crest.

When he described his vision, I could imagine it immediately, as if he had already created it, and I was already there. How incredible, I thought then, to be able to create a world just with words, and then manifest it in this careful, alchemical way. I was quietly enthralled, by the work as well as him.

'Let's meet on Thursday,' he said, in another message. 'The light was so low when we met, I can't remember if you are really as beautiful as I thought, or whether I imagined it. I must have imagined it. It's impossible to be so beautiful. I hope you won't be disappointed in me. I can be quite self-conscious.'

Before our second date, I went out with Nate again to another art opening and met some of his friends. I felt uneasy this time though, in the bright white space again, with people in heavy overcoats and blunt haircuts, smoking their vapes, free beers in hand. I kept fidgeting, thinking of Aidan again, trying to remember as much as I could about him from that one meeting. I had seen his Instagram, all his brooding photographs, his silver mists and shadows. Nate noticed that I was distracted.

'Are you okay?' he asked, and I came back to the room again and smiled, realizing I had been daydreaming so much I was almost dissociating.

'Sorry, just tired,' I replied, but he looked at me quizzically. 'You look hypnotized,' he said. 'Are you on something?'

'No,' I said, feeling self-conscious now.

'Okay.'

It was only later, in another bar, that Aidan's name came up again.

'He broke up with Katie,' another man said. We were all sitting together at a dark wooden table with large glasses of red wine, sharing a bottle. 'She's not doing very well. It was acrimonious. It was very damaging for her, I think. But at least she is out of it all now. She can start to recover.'

There was some muffled agreement, some sideways glances, but all I took in was that he was single, and at that moment he texted me, too.

'Are you still free on Thursday?' he said. 'I can't wait to see you again.'

At night, in bed, I scrolled through more pictures of him; there was a darkness and warmth already, a compulsion in me that he hooked all at once. I tried to convince myself that I wouldn't be so attracted in real life. I tried to tell myself I would be repulsed by him, instead.

He texted me again, sent me an article about masochism and photography and ethics. 'I'm still not sure what I think,' he said. 'Should masochism be pathologized, or is it a harmless thing? I never know how far I should go. But then that is part of the thrill.'

※

We met at a bar called Nachtug and I was there a few minutes before Aidan. When he arrived, he was even taller and more attractive than I remembered, and my heart sank; I was so weak already. He sat down and we ordered Guinness and chatted nervously and then less nervously, as the drink bleached out the angst. The rest of the world fell away, the more we talked; I wanted to be only in his world, the world that opened up when he looked at me, when he spoke – the world that so dizzyingly destroyed my own.

A little later, another drink on, he said, 'I was so nervous to see you again. Could you tell?'

'I was nervous too,' I replied, and we moved closer, but I was still on edge. His intensity drew me in, but it also intimidated me, not because I was scared of him, but because I was scared of myself, by this energy that was already consuming me so deliriously. But I tried not show how I felt; I didn't want him to know he already had me, even though he seemed to assume it in some way. He looked at me as though I were his, and then I was his.

We walked to a Lebanese restaurant after finishing our drinks, in the freezing cold wind. I kept looking over at Aidan as he told me his friends had recommended the restaurant, and he said again that he'd been meaning to go for a while. He liked cooking, he said. 'Me too,' I replied. He told me about a tofu dish he liked to cook, and that he hated all fish except salmon, but that that was it really, he was not particularly sophisticated.

We sat down in the restaurant and ordered red wine, and I worried that I was somehow falling in love with him, out of nowhere, like an idiot. His eyes, his lips, I gazed at them, entranced. And then something far beyond physical things, some unfathomable emotional bond I couldn't understand. We talked and eased into a happy flow until we were both drunk and couldn't eat any more of whatever the waiter brought us, but we just laughed and told stories and deep things casually. Aidan told me that his father had died a few years ago, from liver cancer, after struggling with alcoholism for years; we both kept drinking, even as he described his father's end.

'He went a terrible orange colour,' he said, 'his face gaunt and his eyes puffy and grey, like he had drowned in it.'

'I'm sorry,' I said. 'That must have been very upsetting to go through.'

'I've found it difficult to talk about ever since,' he went on, staring at the table, then looking up at me, forlorn. 'It doesn't feel that long ago. Ever since he died, I've been lost, as if I never know what day it is anymore, because that felt like it was yesterday, but also years ago. I just go around in circles. I can't talk about it though; I can't explain it at all. I shut down when it first happened, didn't know what I could possibly say.' He was talking now, though, and he hadn't known me very long, and yet I didn't say that. It was as if I might have been anyone, really, and he barely looked me in the eye as he talked. And yet, I felt somehow privileged, that the man who said he never talked about his trauma had chosen me to talk to, whether he was fully aware of it or not. He sat very closely, so close I could feel his breath on my cheek.

After dinner, we walked back the way we came, and went to another bar which had no obvious street entrance, just a battered grey door and an intercom. We went downstairs – it was supposed to be a sort of speakeasy but despite the contrived décor, it was fun – and we ordered whiskey cocktails and found a little spot. The mood lightened with the music and then we kissed, and I sank further. Everything else was precarious, but not this desire, I was sure of it. I wanted nothing but him.

We went back to his apartment, a one-bedroom space on the third floor of an old building. Inside there was a mixture of mid-century furniture and familiar IKEA pieces, some sprawling spider plants and orchids, and then various camera equipment and tripods by a large dining table. He turned on a single lamp in the living room. 'Let me just tidy up,' he said, and went into the other room while I sat down on the sofa. I noticed the books he had – mostly art books on Francesca Woodman, Don McCullin, Robert Mapplethorpe. And also some paperbacks – Burroughs, Franzen, Bret Easton Ellis, David Foster Wallace.

He came back in after a little while and sat on a chair opposite me and just looked at me intensely. Although in a way, there was a slight creepiness to his gaze, I went over to him and kissed him, and felt his hand under my shirt, grazing my back, electric. My hair fell over my face, then onto his, and he scooped it up and pulled gently, pulling my head back so that I couldn't kiss him anymore. He looked me in the eye again and said, 'this way' and still pulling my hair, he marched me into his bedroom, pushed me over his bed, then turned me around. He said nothing, just unbuttoned his black jeans, and then my shirt, and then my jeans.

※

I went back and forth from Glasgow, and we went out for meals and drinks together and I sank into a deep infatuation we soon called love. Over dinner, or after sex, we talked about past relationships and our parents and our photography, and other people's work. Glasgow. London. 'It's not for me,' he said about London. 'I could take it or leave it.'

'I prefer Glasgow, too,' I said, and he smiled approvingly.

I fell for him this quickly. The rubble and ice and breaking through, me a little wave, carrying with me a warm expanse of ocean, softly breaking him, melting him. I wanted the dark places, and someone who shared them. He seemed to want that, too. And so there were more dates, and feeling so sure that he was the dream, despite the impossibility of knowing all this in a few weeks. His eyes were sinking pits of tar and I had dreamt of this, I had dreamt of him, someone just like him. And so here I was again. Giddy, panicked, dumb.

I never knew if I was escaping things or trapping myself willingly, whether this was an adventure or emotional bondage. I couldn't make up my mind what I wanted; I was several people, a million desires, and yet they always circled him, or someone who was like him.

❈

Aidan visited me in London twice, staying in the flat I shared in Hackney, but he didn't like my flatmate Robin very much. After the second trip, when he got into an argument with her, he told me that he would rather pay for my train tickets to Glasgow than have to come back to London to see me again, so from then on that's what happened. I would visit him every other week for a few days at a time, sometimes longer, whenever I didn't have in-person work in London.

But the little work I had dried up, and I never found anything lasting, so after a few months of this, Aiden suggested I move in with him, instead of traipsing back and forth. It seemed so straightforward to organize, and so we did. I packed up again, put some things in storage and brought the rest in two suitcases to Glasgow. I took up work as an English teacher for teenagers, and he kept working as a photographer.

The evening that I arrived, I started unpacking more of my things. Rolled up drawings and posters, photo albums. I put a small poster in a frame and hung that. It was a reproduction of an Eduardo Paolozzi print. Intimate, it said, in white cursive writing. CONFESSIONS, in red block letters.

> I was a Rich Man's Plaything.
> Ex-Mistress
> I Confess
> If this be Sin
> Woman of the Streets
> Daughter of Sin

She was a fifties pin-up, wearing a red dress. She wore black strappy shoes and stockings, dark hair.

Real Gold, it said.

Keep 'Em Flying!

A military plane. A smile. Keep 'Em Flying!

A large envelope of old postcards: Toulouse Lautrec, Egon Schiele, and more Paolozzi prints. Buried photos of exes and friends I'd lost touch with. Photos from art school in albums, beneath them. I hadn't looked at them in years. All the scowls and sculking around. Old tickets for movies and exhibitions, letters from friends. Old illustrations. Drawings: a packet of barbiturates, some lilies, a pomegranate, my friend reclining on a couch, book in hand. Evidence of things I could barely remember. A paper trail that led, somehow, to here.

I uncovered some more postcards from an exhibition I had

seen not long ago – the photography of Francesca Woodman. Her body wrapped around, like an eel, with eels. Her image disappearing into thin air. A body that was thin air. I found a clipping of the article I had written about the exhibition, underneath the cards:

> In Woodman's photographs, which she had produced from the age of thirteen until her death at twenty-two, she depicted herself in various situations and poses, exploring issues of gender and the self in relation to its surroundings. She presented the female body – often her own – usually alone, in stark scenes: sitting on a chair in a derelict room, naked except for a pair of black Mary Janes; crouched, in profile, in another sparsely decorated room; naked, again, curled around some eels on the ground.
>
> Woodman presents herself (and sometimes others) as obscured and blurred, using long exposures to create an ephemeral, elusive impression of herself against her static surroundings. As she moves, however slightly, her existence in the photograph is questioned and doubted; her humanity itself, she seems to imply, makes her vulnerable to disappearance.
>
> Woodman was twenty-two when she took her own life. But her photography records an identity and a life, and an experience of life that perhaps seems overwhelmingly ephemeral and elusive at times. They are an act of self-preservation, leaving a record of one's existence despite its inherent precariousness, by containing in single images a sense that a moment of living, breathing, and thinking has been captured and kept, and that these records of living can last beyond the body itself.

I looked at the cards again: Francesca, disappearing. Appearing, disappearing. A vanishing act. She looked how I felt. I thought about the photographs I was now ignoring: my father, Tristan. What was I supposed to do with them all? Was acknowledging them all tipping me into this strange, detached numbness I drifted into so frequently? By looking at them, was I disappearing myself? Deflecting? It all felt the same, one day to the next. The only relief was in seeing Aiden, in being with Aiden. His face – brown eyes, a stern look, the lips with the scar that matched mine, the single hoop – hypnotized me whenever I looked his way, and I had never been happier to be in such a trance.

The city, and the memories and shadows that lingered there, all swirled together in this irresistible way, and so I did fall in love in a way that felt new, special, different – because I was also in love with the city. And while an onlooker might have seen the danger in such intoxicating, and yet false familiarity, I did not. I did not want to see danger; or rather, I did not want to see any danger as something that could possibly come between us.

'People always focus on self-determination,' I told Aiden one morning, as I kept obsessing over this idea, 'and yet one of the most exciting things about life is that it makes you do things you don't intend to do, when things are spontaneous and not always planned out, when things just happen. Life is always submissive and chaotic. We're in denial when we try to act otherwise. Being submissive is merely an acceptance of the chaos of life. Do you know what I mean?'

'I think so,' he said. 'You're trying to validate your desires that still cause you some shame. Because these things might be spontaneous, but they are also planned. You have created a space for abandon.' I wasn't sure if I did feel any shame, though; I wondered if he did about his own behaviour, or if he wanted me to feel that way. It seemed sometimes as though he wanted me to feel more ashamed than I really did, that that would please him more than mere abandon.

'I know there can be shame in compulsion.' I replied. 'But maybe the shame lies not in the compulsion itself, but in a feeling of not having control over the compulsion, of not being able to not want it. I can see why someone might feel that way. I don't think I do though; I just feel anxiety as part of the compulsion, an anxiety about being powerless to it. And so maybe I want a new level of submission. I want a point of submission where I am content in my weakness. Total submission, not merely an act or performance of it. Existential submission. Peace.' He drank his coffee, and I drank mine; it burnt my tongue.

'That sounds like Buddhism, almost,' he replied, quietly.

'Yes, BDSM as a form of Buddhism, why not?'

'But you don't generally need a safe word for Buddhism,' he said, 'and you are not relying on anyone else. So they're not that similar.'

'I know, I didn't mean it like that.' I replied, feeling self-conscious again. He looked at me as if I were deeply idiotic. 'I wasn't being serious,' I went on, protesting in vain. 'I just meant that there is a common desire for some kind of surrender.'

❧

Months passed, with this same sort of back and forth, a building tension between us. One night, we went to a small party that his gallerist was hosting, at a barely renovated flat in a beautiful old tenement building, with the walls still bare and scraped, in shades of grey and dusty pink plaster. The gallerist, Kayla, had put three coffee tables together and laid out various plates of food, though mostly people just drank. As everyone talked about the show, I sank into myself; Aidan seemed to ignore me, enthralled in a conversation with a gallery assistant, who seemed excessively arrogant towards me, though I could not see why. Her manner and voice were clunky, robotic; she spoke with a slight American accent that betrayed International School and transatlantic internships with family friends. She wore her hair tied back in an uneven bun, thick foundation and too much blush, an ill-fitting black dress. She hovered over Aidan, discussing a press list and a price list and he transformed before my eyes into the sort of art world stereotype he usually loathed.

We stayed a few hours altogether, and Aidan became steadily more detached, his eyes become startled; when he began to twitch and stare into space, I called an Uber. When we got home, I put him to bed and then went to sleep as well, but I woke in the night to find him having a sort of seizure - arms flailing, a gone look in his eyes, his nose foaming. I was about to call an ambulance when this suddenly passed.

'Can I call an ambulance?' I asked him, 'Should I?' He didn't react at all for a while, he didn't even see that I was there, even though I was holding him. And yet I didn't phone an ambulance. He calmed down after a few minutes, became gradually more coherent. I was half asleep, confused.

'I'm sorry,' he said, when he finally came round. 'I took too much. You don't need to call anyone. I'm fine now. Go to sleep. I thought you were asleep.'

I couldn't sleep after that, though, and I stayed restless until morning, when the sun rose. I went and made myself some strong black coffee and ran a bath. The tub was a mint green colour, and we had put white candles around the side of it, a small cactus on a wooden shelf above the sink. The tiles were decades old, also a mint green, but it was a peaceful room. I drank the coffee in the bath, both alert and exhausted, on edge. I looked at the locked door and wondered how long I could stay my side of it. This had all been going on for months now, and it never improved; I could see now how much denial I had been in.

'I'll be going out in a bit by the way,' he said later that day, after a prolonged silence. He seemed to have sobered up, and he was wearing an ensemble of baggy khaki trousers and a crumpled black tee-shirt, a silver chain around his neck. He had showered, and his hair was still damp, drying into curls. 'I have to meet someone from the gallery.'

He didn't elaborate on that. I had tried not to be suspicious about his relationships with the people he worked with, the various much younger girls, whom he would meet up with after hours, often pretending to be elsewhere, but I had been proven right too many times. Once he had pretended that he had been at football when he'd been drinking with one of them but came back without his football kit.

Another time he was at drinks with another younger female colleague, pretending it was an older male colleague; I only found out because I received a call from a stranger to say he was passed out in the street, and could I help get him home? The stranger had already tried the girl he'd been with, but she hadn't picked up. When I brought it up with him later, when he had sobered up, he was so furious that he kicked the wall so that a layer of board came off, and a crack appeared. He smashed a wine glass, threw his phone on the floor, and broke that too. He swung a punch at me but missed; then he pushed me onto the bed we shared, trying to strangle me, looking at me as he did so with darkened eyes, until I threw him off. I had caused all this outburst, he said; it was my fault for noticing things. When I flinched days later, he chastised me, for making him feel bad about himself.

'You look at me like I'm some kind of monster,' he said, standing over me. 'But I'm not a monster. I'm not.'

I wished, in a way, that I could not tell when he was lying, but I could, and it was becoming more and more obvious anyway, to the point of absurdity, as if he were testing me, or sabotaging everything on purpose, always assuming I would stay; surer of that, perhaps, the more I put up with. I tried to ignore it, though.

I didn't want to lose him, as he knew, despite all this. It drove me crazy, how nonsensical that was, how desperate really, if I tried to look at it objectively; but I couldn't give in. That would be even worse than what had already happened; then, he would be gone forever, not just an evening or an afternoon.

But as the weeks and then months went on, my mood dropped, and I stayed in the apartment more, or sat in cafés and parks all day. Aidan was focussed on his new exhibition, the photographs of complicated sets and this ambitious installation involving liquid mercury. In the run-up to the show, I barely saw him until the evening of the opening itself, when I met him at the gallery. He had transformed the white cuboid space into a silver one, with a rectangle in the middle that looked like a mirror but was actually a pool of mercury.

On the walls, there were black and white photographs in black frames, featuring little mirrors and smears of powder, doubles and twins and optical illusions. Then there were some images printed or painted onto mirrors themselves – bodies, hands, shadows. I went and gave him a hug; he was shaking.

'You have done so well,' I said, and he looked down as I said this. 'I'm so proud of you,' I went on.

'Thank you.' he said, his eyes fixed to the floor. 'Sorry it's been a stressful time.'

'It's okay,' I replied. 'Everything will get better now.'

More people arrived around 7 p.m. I took a glass of wine from a passing assistant and stepped back as the gallerist and a collector edged in and introduced themselves. I walked around and took a closer look at the work – all these doubles and shadows and smears. I was looking at a self-portrait Aidan had taken in a dirty mirror, his face barely visible, when I heard the splash and then a scream, and turned around – someone had fallen into the silver pool, the toxic mirror, and it was Aidan who was screaming.

'Get him out! Get him out! It's toxic – it's mercury. You weren't supposed to touch the fucking work, let alone dive into it!'

Chaos ensued, with the assistants pouring water on the man's face and stripping his clothes off. Some people thought it was a performance and laughed along, streaming it on social media, until the ambulance arrived.

'Everyone leave!' Aidan screamed, 'it's over; everyone just leave!' But no one did, so he just stormed off into the street, and I followed him out. He didn't want me there though. 'I need to be alone,' he said. 'It's all over. They're going to sue me. It's over, Lena. I need to be alone.'

I stopped walking after him and just stood in the street, watching him disappear. I was so dazed by it all that I didn't notice the motorbike coming round the corner, skimming past me close enough that it knocked me over, unconscious for a few moments. A stranger came over and I woke with my head in their hands, but Aidan had disappeared. I went to the hospital and had an x-ray and some stitches, was told I had a concussion, that it could take a few weeks to subside.

'Do you have anyone to take care of you?' The doctor asked.

'I don't know,' I replied. He looked at me in a way to suggest he wasn't sure if it was the concussion or the reality that had prompted me to say that, but that neither reason was good.

Aidan didn't get in touch for a few days after that. It was upsetting not knowing where he was or what had happened to him, and especially when I was myself injured. Eventually I found out that he had been with another woman the whole time, the repellent gallery assistant of all people; her sheer ugliness I took as a personal slight, an insult to injury as it were, and all this together plunged me into a fresh depression.

A few days later, he tried to make it up to me. He booked a spa day for my recovery; a nice gesture, but ultimately it could not heal me. And yet I found it impossible to let go, as time went on, to let him choose whatever or whoever the current escape was, whether it was a drug or a person or both, over me. He had not really wanted to be gone, either, he said. Things would get better, he said. He didn't know what he had been thinking, he went on; he was sick; he still loved me, always would.

And I wanted all this to be true. But this strained nostalgia was just a way of escaping the present, a desperate attempt to persuade myself that the euphoria of memories might still be recreated. It was a form of denial; every time I repeated or revisited a memory, I was distancing myself on some level, telling the story a little differently, remembering things as somewhat altered, creating a fantasy or fiction that could never be as good as the past, but instead create an impossible standard for the future.

I wondered sometimes if I missed the longing the most, but that wasn't quite right, or at least not the whole picture. I did miss it, though. I missed the yearning, the certainty that something so beautiful was just beyond reach, was just a few days or weeks away. I had been taking photographs throughout our relationship and then they became, with its end, a strange elegy – not only to the old world, long gone, but to that time of romantic confinement itself, and the strange longings and dreams and bizarrely created certainties I had felt then – all the magical thinking that also characterised that early time. I wondered, too, if all along they had also been a coping mechanism, that I had used photography to detach myself in some way, because of course his behaviour and the tension between us had been there for some time and it had always felt intolerable.

Now, everything felt more precarious and fragile than ever. I was hurt. I missed thinking – knowing? – that I would always wake up to the same face, would, after all this, be together with that same person, repeat these scenes. But it was a riddle I couldn't solve. What mattered was the distance, that it was there at all, that it was the wrong sort of distance; not of promise and love but of running away. I missed him all the time, but especially when he was right there, his mind elsewhere.

※

Aidan re-emerged another evening, a few weeks after the accident, bringing food and painkillers, and he fell asleep with me, holding me. I remembered not only the bad times, but all the times he had cared for me, too. My guard was still up, compared to before, and now I was in an opiate haze, but there we were, somehow, together. Even if things would still fall apart, I held him closely, because at least we had this. But then he changed his mind again.

'I don't think it's going to work anymore,' he said. 'I don't think you will ever forgive me. I feel like we can't connect anymore. You won't let me in anymore.'

And it was true; he had hurt me, and nothing I could do would change that. Every time I saw his face on my phone my stomach lurched, even as I longed to be with him. Every time we spent an evening together, I found it harder and harder to speak, until it was just him speaking, and I was just going along with him.

But I was still there, and after a while I began to let him go, surrendering to the stillness of his absence, and the remaining chaos of my own self, which I had known all along, which was nothing to be afraid of after all. I understood why he escaped me, as I escaped him, too, in my way. I tried to see him as free, too, his absence as freeing not cruel. I had loved him, but especially the way the light fell on him. I loved that, remembered that the most, until he was just that, just something light fell onto for a while.

I packed everything I had brought with me to Glasgow, which was not very much, while he was away, and took a train back to

London, where a friend had said I could sublet for a month or so. I turned my phone off for the duration, switching it back on as the train pulled into Euston, and he had not messaged me anyway. But there had been a message from Nate, suggesting I call him, and I put Glasgow and Aidan out of my mind, repeating history without realizing it, finding another side of Scotland to retreat towards instead, another man.

6

NATE HAD PUT together a programme of classes. We were not obliged to go, and yet there was an implication that we should.

'I think you'll like them,' Nate said. 'Adrian runs them. We do them every day, guided meditations. A lot of people find them very helpful.'

Adrian had a certain flair about him. Despite the weather and the location, he always wore a Hawaiian shirt, gold chains, and white or stone-coloured jeans. He had thick-rimmed tattoos of snakes and naked women on his arms and upper chest, pierced hearts by his collar bone.

'Welcome!' he beamed, opening the door to his cottage after several locks that kept it secure. Inside there were potted palm trees and other plants, some red orchids, and the windows were steamed up. He grinned, high, a red vape resting between his clamped, stained teeth.

'Come in, come in,' he said, shuffling us through and bolting the door again. There was soul music playing in the other room and we drifted towards it, through a large kitchen, the counters full of mostly empty bottles of vodka and whiskey, squeezed lemons and empty glasses. Lanterns were strung up from the ceiling and our group of eight lounged over a few tan leather sofas and chairs arranged by some open sliding doors, spilling out onto a dusty terrace. Vape smoke the scent of cherries, raspberries, caramel, and watermelon coalesced in the air with weed and tobacco, hanging over them all like a stale fruity breath.

'Take a seat,' Adrian said, now puffing on his red vape, a cloud of smoke dissipating in the air above him. 'Lena, make yourself at home. Mi casa es tu casa!'

We sat on the floor by the windows, in a circle, and we passed around mugs of cacao and ginger. One girl started humming along to the record – she was skinny with lots of cursive tattoos, a nose ring, and short, bleached hair, some cut off bleached denims shorts, and a crocheted black bikini top.

'I'm super worried about Dan,' she drawled, 'he looked awful this morning.' The others murmured in agreement. 'Like he needs to meditate more, I can't believe I have to keep telling him that. But he just resists, without even realising it. His foot is always tapping.' Adrian nodded slowly, as if he were very wise.

'He'll resist until he breaks,' he said, and the others nodded along with him, but also the music, as if they were seaweed underwater, reacting to the same wave. 'He'll get there though. If he keeps coming along, he'll get there. He's almost ready.'

I had no idea what they were talking about, and just kept drinking the warm and bitter cacao.

Nate puffed on a joint now, hanging decrepit from his lips. The others smiled and murmured in agreement, a soft echo. Adrian gave Nate a manly hug of encouragement and slipped him something else; Nate did the first of many disappearing acts that day.

The afternoon and then evening lingered on in this way, and the soul music changed to an ambient techno, and a few more people arrived as well, including the Priest from before. I noticed as the hours went on that Adrian did most of the speaking; he would tell the others, in a priestly fashion, about his latest readings and the advice he could give them. It was a mixture of Oshi-adjacent texts, Jungian dream analysis and a sort of Buddhism he was apparently developing in a way that was specific to this group and their psychic needs.

He told everyone about the plans he had for the following week. 'We're continuing with the 9 a.m. meditations because they've been so beneficial,' he drawled, still puffing away on the red vape, 'but I'm introducing some new workshops which will fuse psychedelic infusion therapy with inner child work, which will be life-changing for all those who partake. Then, towards the end of the week, we'll be doing some deep sharing, to a soundtrack by Dash here,' he signalled to a man with a beard, cap, and dark glasses, who nodded, beer in hand. 'So that'll be a good, cathartic wind-down after an intense but much needed psychic transformation.'

I looked at Nate as he talked, hoping he would share my own dumbfounded attitude, but he was also nodding along. I realised at this point how dazed he was and wondered if he had even been listening.

'Hey Hana, can you bring some of the food in? I'm sensing depletion.' More nodding, and Hana – a girl with straggly pink hair and a white floral baby doll dress – went to the kitchen. 'Lena, you can go help her,' he said, and I just did as I was told as well. I looked towards Nate as I helped find plates for everyone, but he was not looking in my direction at all; I felt suddenly invisible not just to him but to myself.

Though initially I did not take him up on his offer of the guided meditations, after a while I decided that I might as well, to make it seem as though I was committed to the group. Perhaps some kind of quasi-spiritual practice would be good for me, I started to think, in my more optimistic moments.

The first meditation was a peaceful experience. The group all sat in the same area we had been in before, in a patch of light by the window, and everyone closed their eyes as Adrian spoke. I sat next to Nate and I could feel his breathing next to mine. To my left was Sacha, who wore a black tee shirt and black shorts, and heavy eye make-up. I could feel her breathing too, and I followed that rhythm at first.

'We are in darkness,' Adrian said, very slowly, though we were in light. 'A pulsing blue darkness, beneath the waves of our consciousness. We are asleep to our desires; we react to nothing. In the darkness, the blue darkness, you can feel the energy begin. You may not want to follow it, but it is inevitable. You have no meaningful choice. The blue takes you, very gently, very strongly. This is the gravity of separation, but it will lead to rebirth, to your new, whole self. We are all the same self. Keep breathing as one. We will be free. The pain of separation is only transient, but savour it. It is the seed of your freedom, your deeper love.'

I didn't open my eyes, but lulled into his words, only realising as I did how tense I had been, how much I had longed for guidance. He counted back from fifty, and I heard the numbers stretch out, and I felt the tension ebb and flow, until he said 'zero. Open your eyes.'

And I could see some of the others had been crying, and only then I realised that I had been too. Adrian looked at me approvingly, seeing my smudged mascara, and I felt a sudden nausea, but I suppressed it. The meditation had left me depleted, and yet peaceful.

'Very good,' Adrian said approvingly. 'Very good.'

After that, I went back every day and the meditations were usually the same, or very similar, and I began to feel a need for them. When I was away from Adrian's, I would begin to doubt him and the meditations, but I would also find it impossible to resist going back to them. There was an expectation, a pull to be involved, and in the strange flow state we achieved together. It was as if these sessions structured all of our time there or grounded us in some way; it was a daily routine around which pivoted our activities. I still cooked, and collected the data, and took photographs, and helped Nate with odd jobs, and I went to sit for Hana too, but these sessions provided a space to connect to the land itself, and one another without having to speak.

As I spent more and more time there, I warmed to Adrian. Where once I could not imagine being away from Aidan, now I could not imagine being away from the whole group, and he held us together more than even Nate. Each day, we sat in the light, and then the darkness, and imagined being reborn, so that it felt as if we were, though really it was a sort of limbo.

I became more passive. When I was there, I would do whatever anyone asked of me, finding a peacefulness in obeying orders. I grew fond of the others, too. Hana and I would often cook meals together, and for a time we became quite close. It was not actually the meditations or rituals that bonded us, but sharing out the chores. As she had been there for a while before me, Hana generally took charge, but she appreciated my efficiency. We would put together large meals for everyone using deliveries of misshapen organic vegetables and tinned pulses, vats of root vegetable-based dips and cakes that used almond flour and avocados, sprinkled with rose petals and glazed in honey. As the others talked about spirituality and mushrooms and ketamine, we helped one another pour brownie batter into large tins, pressing in hazelnuts and almonds.

At first, we barely talked, so wrapped up in the food preparation itself, but as we spent more time together, we realised we were both retreating to the kitchen for similar reasons. One day, when the rest of the group were out in the courtyard again, and we heard a glass smash, Hana could not hide her irritation.

'We only have six of those left now,' she said. 'Every day another breaks. We can't really afford that.' Then she corrected herself. 'Never mind,' she said, feigning a relaxed attitude, 'it's just a glass. I'm sure Adrian will take another from a bar or something anyway.' She went to the sink and washed olive oil from her hands, then dried them on a blue towel. Then she let her hair down before putting it back up in a messy bun with a scrunchie. She had dyed it pink at some point, but her dark roots had grown in so much that when she wore it up, the pink section was barely noticeable. She was wearing denim shorts and a long grey shirt, several gold pendants round her neck.

'As long as we don't have to clean up all the glass again,' I said, as that had also happened a few times. 'I didn't care at first, but I got a shard of glass in my finger yesterday and it's really irritating actually.'

'I know, the same happened to me as well. I prefer to wear no shoes, but I can't when there is always broken glass out there. They need to be more careful.' Then we both looked at each other and realised how much we were complaining, and we both smiled.

'Adrian would say we are resisting,' Hana said. 'God forbid we should resist. But probably the hill I'm going to die on is not the broken glass. At least I hope not.' She started folding a towel, and then another, but looked preoccupied.

'Shall we have a break?' I suggested, and Hana smiled again. I went over to the sink and washed my hands - I had been chopping coriander for salads - and I went and sat over at the dining table. Hana brought some fruit and a bottle of wine; I brought two glasses. I was not obliged to drink, of course, but now that I was sleeping and feeling better, and I felt safe in Hana's company, I thought it would be good to attempt some moderation.

'How long have you been here then?' I asked Hana. We had never spoken in much depth at all.

'Three years. I met Adrian here two years ago, and we've been seeing each other since then, in this casual way. His other girlfriend comes and goes, as do other women. I am always surprised it lasted this long, to be honest. I thought maybe a few weeks, in the beginning, but I am still here.'

'Two years seems a long time to be on an island,' I said.

'But time is meaningless,' Hana replied matter-of-factly, 'at least in a situation like this. It is meaningless. One week can feel like a year, and a year can feel like a week. You get sucked in; it is hard to conceive of leaving.'

'I suppose so,' I replied. 'I wanted to come here though, I wanted to stay.'

'Do you still want that?'

'I think so. It has a way of sucking you in, you're right. Or at least Nate did. I don't think I would stay here without him.'

'So you're in love then?' she laughed. There was a hint of sarcasm, but I didn't mind. 'It's the only reason you would be here.' She went on.

'We've been friends a long time,' I replied. 'I think that would ruin everything. I'm not really well enough, anyway. That was the point of coming here, originally. Nate was doing me a favour.'

'Well you seem like you're getting better,' she replied. Hana topped up my wine and then her own. 'It'll all be fine,' she said, in a reassuring way, 'Maybe just serve yourself first, anyway. Don't just focus on any one man, even if he's the reason you came here. We can enjoy ourselves too.'

He was the reason I had come, it was true, but it's not as if I had not wanted to be here for other reasons than Nate – I had been trying to purge myself of other men, for one thing, not to mention my reliance on sleeping pills and alcohol. And in some way, which I think Nate saw before I did, I needed to come back to this part of Scotland as well. It began to irritate me that Hana reduced me to some attachment to Nate, even though we were close. I wondered if she was just assuming my reasons for being here mirrored her own; she had stayed for Aidan for years on this island, and her routines were just as subservient as mine. She had set the tone, really.

'Why are we always the ones in the kitchen?' I asked, then, and Hana smiled again.

'Well, I am there because I want some space, I get bored doing nothing. I don't want to lie around on psychedelics all day. And I just like cooking. Why are you here?'

'I wasn't sure. That's why I asked you.'

'Well perhaps you need to figure that out for yourself then. You haven't been here that long.' She looked at me directly, then. 'Maybe you want to get away from them. Maybe you love my company? Or maybe you just like cooking too.'

'Maybe all those reasons' I replied. 'And I like the smells. Sometimes it is nice to smell fresh fruit instead of cherry vape smoke or tobacco.' And yet we could still smell it, along with the ever-present acrid smell from the birds outside, though I didn't mention that. It was their island, after all. It seemed rude to comment.

Later, after everybody had eaten the salads, flatbreads, and dips we had made, I went and sat with Nate, thinking about what Hana had said. He was laying out on a small futon in a patch of sun by the window, and I curled into him, as I often had before, though he seemed rigid compared to usual. Then I smoked a cigarette and drank more wine, happy to have the sun bearing down on me and wiping me out. I kept drinking, then gravitated back towards Hana, both of us in a blur now.

As night gradually fell, the skies alive with scorching pinks and ambers, we talked more. The rosy sheen of sunset lightened our perceptions; I wanted Hana to know that my love for Nate was a good thing, that attachment was not merely something else to discard in some quest for spiritual growth.

'You know we were quite young when we met, Nate and I? We met at twenty or twenty-one, at a friend's funeral. It is special to be friends all these years later.'

'That is nice,' she agreed, now resting on a floor cushion, in a patch of light, her eyes closed.

'How did you meet Aidan?' I asked. She had only told me vaguely before. I wanted to know why she liked him enough to stay through so many winters here.

'It started as an art project,' she said. 'I had a grant to research a short film about birds, and he was already here. He was very eager for me to come, said he knew my work already. He helped me fill out the application. But we had never met until I arrived here. And within days I knew I would stay longer than the project. This place was so much bigger than me; I began to care for it in a way I had never cared about anything else in my life. I had not been happy before, but here I began to forget whole lengths of time. Now I barely remember my teenage years, I barely remember my early twenties. I haven't seen my parents since I arrived.'

I had been expecting a rosy story of love, but Hana began to disturb me.

'What do you mean you don't remember anything?' I asked.

'Well, I think – maybe because I wanted to forget for so long, that eventually I did. I can't remember the years before here. I just remember the better times since arriving.'

I wasn't sure how to respond, and she sensed my unease. 'Do you remember your childhood well?' she asked me. I thought about it; it was hard to say. Maybe it was similar to her experience in that way.

'I remember some things.' I replied. 'But I wish I remembered more. I wish I could remember more about my father. I think it's one reason I like being back on the North East coast; I feel closer to him here. I remember more, just skies I must have seen when I was younger, a feeling of space. Sometimes the way Nate and Aidan walk around, even, it reminds me of him too.'

'Memory is so strange,' she replied. 'Sometimes you do need other people to make sense of it, to reconnect or disconnect from what matters, or doesn't anymore. You know what we should do next?' she asked, her tone suddenly brighter, as she moved herself up to the foot of the couch, looking directly at me now.

'What?'

'You can sit for me, for a portrait. I've already painted everyone else. It's a rite of passage, you could say.'

'Sure,' I said, without thinking about it. 'What do I have to do?'

'Just sit there, very still.' She smiled, untying her hair and then putting it back up in a bun.

'I think I can do that.' I replied.

'It's actually harder than it looks, but I think you can too. Come round tomorrow or the next day, we'll start then.'

As the evening wound on, and Adrian started handing around cups of his mushroom tea, I asked where it was all coming from, and were there mushrooms growing naturally on the island?

'No,' Adrian said firmly. 'But they are growing in our attic. Perfect conditions, really. It is a time of growth, for the island and for us. Try some, if you like? It's very weak tea, you'll be fine.'

I did as he suggested, sipping the earthy tea, which looked a deep red only because it was served in red cups. At first, I noticed no difference, but as time went on, everything around me appeared slightly more luminous than before, as if lit up by candles. I lay with Hana and Nate on the rough grass, between our cottages and the cliffs, staring at the night sky, at the stars. There were three up there together in their constellation, all those light years away from each other and from us, in the same pattern we were resting in now. I lay on Nate's shoulder, convinced that everything was just as it should be.

7

I FOUND THE first dead bird the last Tuesday of May, in the middle of one of the pathways, a metre from the cliff edge. I made a note of it and left it be, not thinking anything much of it. The following day, Sara found two dead gulls on another path, though, and then the next day there were five by the edge of the lagoon. We made notes and didn't think much of it until the next week, when there were a hundred dead birds all over the island. This was when Nate started making some calls, and we started paying more attention to what appeared to me some kind of avian flu. 'There's no need to panic,' he said, 'we just need to make a note of everything we see. This is Mother Nature; all we can do is observe.'

As the days went on, more bones and full carcasses started washing up on the shore; I'm sure I imagined it, but it seemed as if the gulls' cries were shriller than usual, sharing the news amongst themselves, warning others. And as they cried out to one another, we took notes for the researchers, made a tally of deaths each day, and left the corpses well alone. Sometimes, in the meditations, their images would intrude upon me, but I let them leave me again, in this ebb and flow of death, the tide coming in incrementally, as we watched from our cottages on the cliff.

As it got worse, we realised we needed a system, and one person taking responsibility for it, and that fell on me, simply because Nate decided it would.

'Lena,' he said, one morning over breakfast, 'you can be in

charge of collecting the data. You can compile and check it every day, check everyone's observations, and send it all to the researchers. That is your new job.'

We tried to put it out of our minds, to let nature take its course. We tried not to touch any of the birds. We tried not to panic. We put our efforts in other things, in emptying our own minds, and those of one another. I balanced my time between scouring for dead birds, checking the data, taking photographs of the cliffs and fauna, going to meditations, and sitting for Hana.

※

As Hana drew me, I began to give in to my feelings and lack of feelings, the ebb and flow of emotion, sensation, and disembodied thoughts. It started to feel like meditation, in a sense. I felt medicated by the stillness. I caught her eye and then looked back at the smudge of grey on the wall, my visual anchor for today. I breathed, moving ever so slightly as I did so, feeling the hard wood of the chair against my back, my right leg going numb, and with that, the temptation to move, ever so slightly. A temptation to itch, and a determination not to.

My mind wandered to Aidan, to recent events, these splintered memories, and then I would be brought back to the present. 'Eyes' she said, and I remembered that I was being drawn, and I looked back at the wall again. I was fixing on a tiny, barely-there smudge, below a dark wooden shelf, about a metre from where I was sitting. We were in the kitchen, a little kitchen, and I was looking in the opposite direction to where the light got in, or rather, about a ninety-five-degree angle.

As Hana sketched, we talked, and I tried to remember to keep looking at the wall. But my instinct was always to look back to her at some point, to laugh and meet her gaze, even though she was busy drawing anyway, and rarely met mine back, focussed on something just to the side – like my nose or my eyebrow perhaps, I never really knew. When she did make eye contact occasionally, I laughed, as if this was a rule broken, an accidental subversion.

I was not typically a model, or a subject. I was usually in the other role. This was my first sitting, and it was a challenge. I struggled to sit still, at the best of times. And now, it was really the worst of times, and yet this seemed as good a time to sit still, or try to, as any. I had been feeling so dissociated and strange that in a way it was perfect for just sitting here, doing nothing. Perfect for being told what to do, which was at once very little, and a huge effort, and then nothing at all again. I kept my eyes open but saw nothing much at all. Occasionally, I heard Hana rub something out. I imagined being rubbed out, that image of me, and it was a pleasing thought.

I remembered Aiden again; that was one of the things that bonded us, in the beginning. We could erase one another, or rather, we allowed each other to feel erased, gone – holding one another in our arms. We took turns, changed things up, let ourselves go, let each other go. This dance of emptying ourselves of memories, of life, of sadness – until what this was, what we did, consumed us. But I loved it. He loved it. It was the ultimate freedom, the ultimate trust. To disappear in another's arms. To exist just as emptily as we wanted. To trust we would be caught. I had longed for it all my life. That connection, the seeming real love, the tortured love, as it would come to be. A 'trauma bond' as the psychology websites would tell me, later on, when things began to unravel. When things had begun to hurt, to go numb, beyond control. But then that – the control, who had it – was often up for debate.

I had drawn a picture of Aidan once, in the early days. He was lying in his bed, with bars like a jail behind him, sheets around him, in a foetal position. I worshipped him; every kiss, every sacrifice, an act of devotion. He was a lost thing, too. We would agree, blissfully, that we had saved one another, wrapped in each other's arms.

'Eyes,' Hana said. I was distracted again. I looked back at the smudge on the wall and she said, 'thank you,' and kept drawing. She looked at me and I looked at the wall. The sadness swelled up and it still made no sense and perhaps it never would. Perhaps I would never feel better. Maybe this devastation would linger, pointlessly, forever, and I wouldn't ever be able to fight it or accept it or assuage it. This pain would last forever.

I kept staring at the smudge on the wall, which served to rebalance me, unthinkingly - to punctuate the waves of emotion, reminding me it existed, too. The smudge on the wall existed just as the pain did, and it didn't go away, it remained there. And Hana kept drawing - me, or rather, the light on me, the way the light fell on me, an object, a living, breathing thing. I dissociated, automatically, and in this one flickering moment, the pain was gone.

'That was very good today,' she said at the very end, after three hours of sitting in one position. 'How did you find it?'

'Quite hard, but I expected it to be. My back is a bit numb. It felt like a long meditation, something like that. It was very peaceful, even though it was difficult. It's a relaxing space here, you know.'

'Thank you. I like to work in here. The light is always good.'

I yawned and stretched; the light was in fact disappearing now. Hana started putting her pencils and sketchbook away. 'Would you like a cup of tea or anything?' she said. Instinctively, I looked around for alcohol, but there didn't seem to be any. She seemed to read my mind and smiled.

'Would you like a cup of tea?'

'Okay, thanks,' I said.

'How has your sleep been lately?' she asked, and I realised I must be looking as tired as I felt.

'Not that great. I keep having nightmares about my ex. It's frustrating, and I can only blame myself.'

She looked sympathetic. 'You've just been unlucky. You've had a string of damaging relationships, but it doesn't always have to be this way.'

'But I always end up in the same place. It is like an addiction, but I don't even know what I'm addicted to, really. I don't go out of my way to find these men. They just gravitate; I can't explain it.'

'Each time,' Hana said, 'you must think that things will work out differently, but they won't. And yet you have some connection with them, I get that. You are operating on the same frequency, I think. They can see you a mile off, you're right; you assuage all their problems, and for the briefest time, or maybe longer, I don't know, they help you escape your problems too. So you're medicating one another. But it's not real love if that is the primary bond. It is like an addiction. Your only possibility of regaining control is leaving. But not being so scared of what you'd have to face by yourself, that you'd go right back.'

I felt deflated as she said this; with Aidan, it had all felt real. It had felt like love. I desperately wanted a drink, then, as a panic arose in me again, but she gave me tea instead.

'Whenever I have a break-up, even if I haven't been drinking or anything before, then it's all I want,' I explained. 'I really find it impossible otherwise.'

'I know, but it'll make it worse. The last thing you need is to drink yourself into oblivion. That's the point of being here anyway, one of the points.' I started crying, then, unaware I had been on the verge of it.

'I'm sorry,' I said. 'This is so embarrassing.'

'It's not,' she said, more quietly, pausing her drawing. She seemed to edge closer for a moment, perhaps to offer a hug, but then moved back. She went back to drawing.

'I think they are happy to see me so sad.' I went on, knowing as I kept talking that I was probably annoying her, but feeling some need to explain myself to her, or them to her, or to myself.

'Your sadness is just a mirror for theirs.' She replied, now putting her pencils away, moving her chair to the side of the room.

'But they are making me sadder. And I feel like I have no control over it, over what they do. That is what I keep coming back to.'

'But you gave your power away to them,' she said. 'Sometimes, in good faith perhaps.' It irritated me that she said this though; it had not always been true. I had not been thinking of power; I had just been consumed by love. I had not been thinking at all. 'But these are not men to give power to.' She went on, ignoring whatever irritation I was radiating. 'You need to start saying no to them.'

She moved the chair I had been sitting on and started clearing things away, and I understood it was time to go. Three hours of silence and restraint, only to burst into tears at the end. I wiped my eyes, feeling idiotic for it, for this lack of control. And yet I felt comfortable with her and she didn't really seem to mind, or if she did, I felt I could push further.

'What's the point though?' I asked. 'They do what they want anyway. Why not just give in? At least them there is a semblance of autonomy on my part.'

'Except there isn't. Look at you now.' She seemed irritated with me at last, or at least frustrated. 'The autonomy you have now is simply to leave, to stop being manipulated, over and over again. Stop making it so easy for them. Stop taking their wounds as your own.' I wondered if she was talking specifically about Nate now, but I didn't ask. He kept crossing my mind and yet I could not resist those thoughts either; to voice them would be to ruin them too soon. I did want him, of course I did. But to say it out loud to Hana would be to turn that feeling into a choice, which would mean I might have to say no. I preferred him as a presence in my mind, a person in my bed, below words or thought.

I just said, 'I know' instead and drank up the rest of my tea. Hana seemed satisfied with this answer, no longer irritated. I had conceded she was right. And she was, anyway. I was misguided, emotional, weak; I was not unaware of that. But these flaws gave me some enjoyment, that was also true. I settled into the familiar dynamic again anyway, with Hana now; in a dance of mutual understanding and evasion, I felt at home.

'Same time tomorrow?' she asked moments later, as I went to leave.

'Yes of course. See you then. Thank you.'

I went back to the cottage in a strange mood and Nate was there. He had been cleaning the kitchen and dried his hands in a towel as I came in.

'Can I help with anything?' I asked, but he said no. He had a roast chicken in the oven, which smelled good already. He had lit two dark candles on the table.

'How was the sitting?' he asked me, as I sat down on the sofa and he put some plates away.

'It was harder than I thought it would be,' I replied. 'My legs kept going numb. But I liked it; it felt meditative. I like Hana, too.'

'That's good,' he said. 'I thought you two would get along.'

He came over and sat next to me, picking up a notebook with things we had to do; it was just in this mundane moment I realised that I had fallen for him in some way, much deeper than I realised, and it overwhelmed me all at once. I did not want to be in love, and yet I had always loved him. But this was not supposed to happen.

I moved away from him slightly, against my instinct to move closer; I asked tepid questions about the island that I was sure would bore him, hiding away from us both. He wrote down a long food list, asked me if there was anything out of ordinary with the birds.

'Nothing really, just the same as yesterday, a few more. It's all in the document though.'

He stood up then and went to the oven, took out the chicken, and let it sit for a while as he prepared a salad. I wanted to talk more about the birds, but it seemed wrong to do so when we were about to eat one, and for a moment I had a horrible thought that it was not a chicken he had cooked, that it was another bird; but I pulled myself together and quietened my own paranoia. I knew he wouldn't do something like that without asking at least.

Later, we ate together, and he told me more about his family; his brother he hadn't seen in a few years and his mother who lived in America now.

'The last time I saw her was on New Year's Day three years ago, and we had another argument,' he said. 'I just couldn't do it anymore; it wasn't even an important argument; I can't remember what it was. But I just couldn't see her again, I couldn't do it after that.' He took a sip of wine, which had now become routine again. 'It's been a relief, honestly. To have a place like this. The people here. I know Aidan can be a bit much, but he is always here, he is a good friend.'

'I know,' I replied. 'I'm glad you have all this.'

'You do now as well,' he said, clearing the plates, and I realised he had brought me into his family, he had given me a home. Perhaps that was why I felt so close and so indebted to him; it was the only thing I had ever really craved, and he had too, and he had created it for us both. This was a kind of love.

Hana had a pencil and a rubber and drew standing by the door, this time, instead of sitting. We were in the kitchen again, and she had moved the chair into the right position – the same as before – as I sat on it. Now, I could see her only in the corner of my eye, as I kept facing the wall. She held the pencil in her mouth sometimes.

'Back', she said, 'to me a little,' she said. 'Thank you.'

I asked her who else she drew, and if she ever drew anyone asleep, as surely that would be easiest?

'I once drew my father asleep,' she said, 'without him knowing. But he was a bit self-conscious about that. Eyes,' she reminded me, and I looked back at the wall.

When we took a short break, about an hour later, I remained sitting as she made some raspberry tea. There was incense twirling through the air, and a bottle of red wine, half full, and postcards of birds and wildlife. There was a candle with a cherub on it, some wilting pink roses, and a yellow and green plant. I could just see a glimmer of her reflection in the window to my left – forcing me to remember myself again. Sitting here had so far been a practise of forgetting myself, drifting off. Sitting with myself was sitting in a daydream; it was noticing myself as an object amongst many.

I went back into the pose, and Hana started drawing again, after I'd had a glass of water. I noticed the details on the chair in front of me, on which a blue jacket was hanging – the carving, the swirls pronounced and jutting out, a feminine, sturdy thing.

My eyes stung, tired from the night before. I had been drinking and smoking; the haze lingered still, and I yawned. As the minutes and hours went on, my back grew numb. My hands and arm hurt, and especially my knee hurt, from the accident. I kept biting my lip, dry from the cold. I could hear the gulls squawking in the distance.

'I'm dancing around you,' Hana said, 'but I'm almost there. I think I've got it. I think I can see it now.' I looked over at her, remembering she was drawing me again. 'It's going to be a painting,' she went on. 'Full length, just like this. I like the black – like that . . . Keep wearing that black jumper.' It was a black cashmere rollneck, which Aiden had bought me our first Christmas together. The trousers were a more recent acquisition, but they had a rip in the left knee, from the accident. They told their story, though I didn't mention the specifics to Hana. Nevertheless, it was fitting. I agreed to keep wearing the same clothes each time.

The first sitting, we had talked a lot, even though I was hungover and concussed, but this time, I already felt less disorientated, and we talked less, and I felt I was getting better at sitting still. Hana said it was coming back to her too, the drawing, that she was getting faster now, it was coming more naturally, with each time. I felt completely unselfconscious when she was drawing me too, more so with each sitting. Sometimes I thought I was completely in my body, and other times my mind drifted, but it didn't matter if I just stayed still for her.

'You have quite a unique bone structure,' she said, the third or fourth sitting, 'but I'm getting there. Very soft features, but a strong structure.' She would not let me see the drawing, though, evading my attempts to catch a glimpse, as I sipped water during a break. She laughed, shutting the sketchbook closed.

'This reminds me of my ballet teacher,' I told Hana a little later. 'He used to make us all stand with our arms outstretched for an uncomfortably long time. It felt torturous; it was actually a stress position, I think. But after a while I kind of enjoyed it, the peacefulness beyond the pain. It was strangely relaxing, to be so disciplined. I became much stronger from it, as well.' Hana smiled a little and kept drawing.

Later, we talked about the artist-subject relationship more generally, how in some cases it built up and continued over years. 'It is similar to psychoanalysis in that way, isn't it?' We'd mentioned it before, when Hana was talking about Lucien Freud, but the more this went on, the more the stability and security of that rhythm became more obvious. 'And I suppose it makes sense, since Lucien was Sigmund Freud's grandson. Perhaps something rubbed off.'

Another sitting, she played classical music, and I remembered those ballet lessons again, the soft absence of talking, this time. Of being supervised, in a way – watched – and kept in line. And yet the freedom, the passive caring nature of that. She was teaching me to be still; I was showing her how light fell on me, specifically, letting her see me in ways I did not even see myself. It was a sort of dance, or a lesson, or something.

I gazed around the kitchen again, as much as I could without moving, and I felt content to be there, in this space, perhaps the most domestic of all spaces, as the light gradually mellowed, and the hours went on. I remembered meeting Nate before in Glasgow and how this had reminded me of that, because we had so often sat in his kitchen as well – drinking coffee in the mornings and chatting and then just sitting again, and in a way, he had also taught me to be still, when I was finding it very hard to do so at all. I remembered how, recently, I had called him when things were at their very worst. How I had seen him all the time, sat with him in his kitchen quite frequently, letting the hours pass, letting him decide what we did, whenever I was with him, and how caring that had been.

Nate had said I was an easy guest to have, back then anyway, because I could just sit there, and we didn't necessarily have to talk, and I could just be part of the furniture. And here I was again. My back was so numb I felt perhaps I had grown into the chair I was sitting on, becoming so numb, and so safe, that I was a part of it now. The light fell on me no differently.

But at night-time, in bed by myself, it felt less blissful, and less easy to become a thing, to be still and meditative. Yearning bled into pessimism and despair. The pain was too much again, and though I had intended not to, I started drinking again. And as Hana had said, it made it worse, and yet I kept drinking. Even after what had happened, I still loved Aidan, at least it felt that way – and the alcohol let me wallow in those feelings that the rest of the time I told myself were wrong. I missed him; the pain of being discarded still stung. The alcohol was not enough, then pills were not enough, then nothing was enough. The sadness would not be contained by any of it; it consumed every attempt at joy.

It was not only these past memories that were keeping me up at night now, but also the birds, or rather their smell. We had all developed an unspoken rule not to dwell on that any more than we had to, and I wondered if that was why everyone began to drink more freely, to light the fires even though it was the middle of summer, to let our lungs fill with smoke instead of death, to distract ourselves with more and more tasks, endless cleaning and documenting.

With all this going on, I continued to turn up for the sittings nevertheless, and as I sat there in Hana's silence, I remembered more and more from my relationship with Aidan. Betrayals that had stacked up, to a point where I had separated from myself, buried myself anyway, in an attempt to get a handle on it, to have any chance of accepting or understanding what had happened. In no longer recognising any of these men, because their actions had not aligned with the idea I had had of them, I had ended up no longer recognising myself either. I didn't trust anything or anyone at all, and merely medicated myself enough to tolerate life in small doses.

But gradually, now I was away from that, on this island, I tried to let myself surrender, stop trying to make sense of what was senseless, to stop trying to understand what still felt ruthless, a collection of myriad betrayals I held close. I tried to allow myself to give up all hope, instead; to allow the sadness to swell inside me, settling in its own sort of stillness. As if I lay on the bottom of an ocean, I tried to let it take me, instead of them. At least this despair was my own, it was a private thing that could not be taken from me.

Chaos had not proven a great friend, and yet depression, at times, seemed to protect me. In some way, I had to learn to trust it rather than anyone else. To sit there, to simply sit there, to be drawn as closely and accurately as possible, to be seen in a plain way. This was the one time where I was told what to do, and I felt safe, contained. I just sat there, as she told me to, and I was safer and freer than I had been in some time.

❦

The next day, I found it easier to sit, to fall back into the pose. We listened to folk music this time and talked about ways of perceiving and remembering things, how everyone remembered things differently. Hana asked me if I had been working on anything on the island, myself.

'I've taken some photos, but I have no particular project in mind,' I said. 'For me, I think I photograph to remember things properly, as if I'll forget them if I don't. They're like prompts,' I explained. 'I'm not sure what I'll do with them later.'

In the way Hana painted, she was also layering memories, creating them in real time, as accurately as possible so that the past had never fully gone. And yet here, right now, I kept having to be present for her; if I was not present, not remembering to be still, then the drawing would capture that sort of absence, too, a person stuck in the past.

We sat in silence for another two hours, and I became anxious towards the end, as if even talking about remembering things had triggered memories I did not want. Taking photographs was often a way to remember things as I wanted to remember things, not as they were, and yet often a certain mood would filter through unconsciously, whatever I intended.

Sitting here, I kept remembering pictures I had taken, and then nightmares I had had, which had become more frequent lately, despite the extra sleeping pills I had been taking to quell them. I kept trying to return to the chair I was looking at, and to Hana, but I was drowsy. Hana drew past my mood, looking at my face, and I realised my thoughts were invisible. But this contradiction of inner and outer worlds seemed strange to me.

The more I sat, the more the memories returned, those I had avoided – not just recent things with Aiden, but also years ago with Tristan. This present pain had been compounded by that past, and it was hard to see a way out. I had always looked to art and friendship as an antithesis to this, but in this very moment, as everything hurt, as I struggled to keep still, to breathe, I wondered if it could ever be enough. I sat through it though, as Hana played some music, classical mostly, gradually those memories were less present, less intense, and I found myself meditating on the mark on the wall once again, until the three hours were up.

'That was really good today,' she said, afterwards. 'Well done.' I just smiled, and I wondered if she had any idea what I had been thinking or feeling, whether any of it had come across, or whether I had just been very, very still.

At the next sitting, we didn't talk very much, but I thought about how a self is always a collaboration; that we cannot be ourselves without one another. And what I had been afraid of was losing that connection; it was why I couldn't really comprehend losing Aidan before, it was why I still missed him sometimes, even now. Every relationship was a creation between two people; we had worked on this one together, every day, and the thought of it being over, completely, seemed impossible. I did not want to stop working on it. I didn't want the idea that we had, the reality of things, to be disappearing. But I realized I couldn't control it; that was the point. It was a joint endeavour. It required a joint effort to persist. In being forced to be still now, to play that part in this new, different collaboration, where I couldn't even see the drawing that Hana was working on, I learnt to surrender myself to the process a little better.

As I walked back to the cottage afterwards, I couldn't shake a sudden sadness, though, a feeling of vulnerability. Even though Hana had been the different to others, and I had been so safe with her in this situation, I had also felt everything I couldn't feel before, just by sitting there. She expected nothing else of me. The stillness of sitting for Hana had opened up the depth of my sadness, for a stillness I struggled to find anywhere else.

I could see now it was me, just as much – addicted to sensations and stimulations, to moving, roaming, impossible men, because they enabled me to be those things myself, they enabled this mutual escapism. We had mirrored one another; they had pierced me like one pressing a finger into a still lake, revealing endless movement.

8

EACH DAY, I would get up at 6.30 a.m., and begin my walk around the coast of the island. It was difficult, of course, because there were so few accessible beaches; mostly, the cliffs were so high that I would have to try and peer down below, ignoring my natural vertigo to do so. But I had good eyesight, and so despite the difficulty of the job, I was able to crouch on the cliff edges, and count dead birds from there. Sometimes, it was much easier anyway; when the birds dropped dead mid-flight, or keeled over on the rocks, I could more easily count them.

I was not to move the birds, and so they began to litter the island; they died at a quicker pace than they decomposed or washed away, and the scent of their death lingered as long as their bodies did. Though I pushed the sight of their corpses out of my mind, I couldn't ignore their smell, even at the cottage. I suggested we bulk buy candles whenever someone was next on the mainland, and Nate agreed.

In those early days, even though I saw so many of the dead birds, I did not think any of it affected me particularly; in hindsight, I think I merely became desensitised, and buried my concern. And perhaps that is why I started sleeping with Nate; maybe my anxiety was so subconscious that I sought comfort in him without fully realising why. Living in such close proximity and with so much shared history, perhaps it was only a matter of time anyway; intimacy was its own kind of contagion, easily spread, and easily taken.

What was funny was that after so much talking about each other's previous relationships, we hardly discussed our sexual turn. We just kissed on the sofa, when the others had left, and found that it was warmer to sleep together than in our separate beds, and then it turned out that all along, in some way, mostly subconscious, we had wanted each other. That was natural, surely? Maybe it was true what people said, that men and women could never really be just friends. I had lost my senses in every other way, so perhaps this was inevitable too. Though we didn't tell anyone else anything, they could already tell. When I went to my daily sitting with Hana, she brought it up once so matter-of-factly.

'I always knew you two would get together; it happens every time,' she said, as she rubbed something out.

'Every time?' I asked. I knew by her tone she meant something of it.

'Every time there is a new helper, a new recruit. It happened to me and Adrian, it happens every time. You come to the colony; you get colonised.' I didn't love how she put it, but I was still giddy from the pleasure, and it was true anyway.

'Stop smiling,' she said. 'A smile distorts the face.'

'You want me sadder.' I replied.

'Exactly', she said, suppressing her own smile this time.

Due to the birds' illness, the researchers asked us to put certain protocols in place. As well as recording the deaths, and avoiding touching the birds, we had to sanitise our cottages and the street that connected them, as well as the research centre itself. I mixed bleach and water and threw buckets over the cobbles, and cleaned all the surfaces inside, and then I went to help the researchers too, though they were away whenever I went to visit them, spending more time away than before.

The boats would come back and forth as usual, and we had the usual food deliveries, but the fishermen left everything at the harbour and then set off more quickly than they had when I first arrived. Two of the group, Dan and a girl I had never even spoken to, left together one early morning without saying why, but Nate told me not to dwell on it, and that the island was a naturally transient place, where people migrated back and forth just like the birds.

Life went on, anyway; there were always new tasks. With each delivery, we had to carry the boxes quickly up to the cottages, storing everything carefully before preparing the meals. It was concerning, of course, that the deaths kept rising, and yet Nate and Adrian never seemed alarmed; they just added more bottles of whiskey to our food order and told us that this was nature's way, and it would all be over in a season.

In many ways, I was happiest in this time, because Nate and I were closer than ever. Though I knew we were mainly friends, and we could never let ourselves ruin the friendship by letting our feelings stray out of control, I found myself more content than I had been in months, so at ease in the casual intimacy we had found on this beautiful island, even if its other inhabitants suffered from a sickness we could not fathom.

This might all have been blissful, the final manifestation of our utopian project, had Nate not begun to transform in an unexpected way. In hindsight, I think the plight of the birds must have upset him more than he let on, and he became moodier than I had ever known him to be, always just containing his anger, which threatened to spill out.

In the cottage, he was more domineering, and I wasn't sure why; he created new rules for me to follow, in the kitchen and in the bedroom, and though I did not complain, it all began to wear me down. If I did anything wrong, his sense of disappointment crushed me. And the more I disappointed him, the more anxious and distracted I became, and then I did make mistakes. I peeled the eggs wrong, or I cut the herbs wrong, or I dropped things; it was as if I began acting out the ways he told me not to, even though the last thing I wanted was to disappoint him. But I knew he had an ideal that I was failing to live up to; some resentment that he did not want the real me began to fester.

When Hana told me what to do in the kitchen, she did it respectfully and it was always an easy, playful atmosphere; I didn't mind at all, because we were both working as one. But when Nate started telling me what to do in this new domestic sense, I found it jarring and myself out of kilter. His tone was different; he found tiny things to pick me up on. In bed, too, I began to resist without meaning to; I did not want to do everything he wanted me to do, and I found myself tensing up, beginning to object, to find dismay where he found pleasure.

But he would just find some other boundary to push – mentioning other girls he could sleep with instead of me, if he wanted to, bringing Hana into every scenario, which confused me of course.

'It's just part of the role play,' he said, when I looked hurt, then, because he was intruding on our own friendship in a way that seemed wrong. 'You shouldn't go along with things, you know. I would feel terrible if you were doing anything you didn't want to do. That would really upset me.'

But sometimes I didn't know if this taunting and confusion was part of the role play or not – whether I was being punished for his pleasure or because I had done something wrong. It all began to feel the same.

My sleeplessness worsened after that, and most nights it would take several hours to fall asleep. And then when I did finally drift off, I'd wake soon after from nightmares. One night Nate shook me awake because I was crying in a dream; it took a moment to realise what was happening, that I was safe with him.

'It's fine,' he said. 'You're with me now, you don't have to be scared anymore.' He held me as my breathing calmed down and then stroked my hair, holding my head into his chest. When I was breathing normally again, he went away and brought me a glass of water and a sleeping pill and then I slept better after that, even though a part of me was disappointed in myself, that the rehabilitative element of this project was failing.

The following morning, we went back to Adrian and Hana's cottage, and Nate encouraged me to tell Adrian what had happened. We were sitting around the concrete dining table this time, and Adrian was peeling an orange.

'Night terrors are a classic PTSD symptom,' he said, with an air of superiority, after I briefly described my experience. 'Unresolved trauma can be torturous.' He offered me some of his orange and I took it; the sour juice burst in my mouth. I sipped some water afterwards; he kept eating the segments and I wondered if they were as sour as the piece I had had.

'I've found that mushrooms can really help rewire the brain after trauma,' Adrian continued. 'But it's best to be in a consistent, supportive environment. So, if you'd like, we can guide you. We had Sacha do a ritual only a few weeks ago – it was a similar situation to this – and she's doing a lot better now. So, the option is there if you'd like. You don't have to go through this alone.' His gaze never left me as he talked; he barely blinked. His eyes were a crystalline blue.

'Sure,' I heard myself saying. 'If you think it would help.'

Adrian broke into the loveliest smile, then, and said 'sweet,' and Nate seemed happy with my compliance as well.

'We'll both sleep better,' he said. 'I'm bored of hearing about depression. I'm bored of depression itself. I want us to both be well, you know. That's all I want.'

I was taken aback by the coldness of his tone, but then I

thought about it and I agreed. Depression bored me too; that was what it was. It bored me so deeply, entrenched itself so stubbornly, and yet I could always look the other way.

'It'll be fine,' Adrian said, getting up from his metal chair. 'Depression and trauma are states we all have to move through – sometimes alone, sometimes together. But it's a chance for growth, it's a chance for awakening. It's a gift.'

Later, we all lay out in our meeting space, the stones feeling baking hot in the surprise midsummer sun. I was wearing sunglasses, but it was still too bright, so I put a towel over my eyes as well. Adrian was playing ambient techno and smoking a cherry vape again, drinking a Peroni from their latest haul from the mainland.

'What does the ritual involve, then?' I asked, and it took a while for Adrian to respond.

'It's just a dose of mushrooms,' he said, 'but in the room we light the lanterns and keep everything soft, and then as you explore your memories, I'm there to guide you. That's all it really is. Sometimes we add sound bowls as well . . . We can do it this evening,' he went on. 'It's better in the evening, when the light is low, and we can have candles as well. It's a better atmosphere.'

I waited until the evening, and Hana said she would join me too. We only took a small amount of mushrooms and lay on blankets on the floor, wrapped in more blankets, our heads resting on linen-covered cushions, over Persian rugs. Adrian had lit candles at the edges of the room, and the charcoal grey blinds were down, so only the faint glow of dusk appeared round the edges, a sliver of gold seeping through. The lanterns were glowing, strung up from the beams of the roof, and only now that I was lying down, did I notice that the ceiling was painted black.

'Close your eyes,' Adrian said, 'and focus on your breathing. Be mindful of the warmth of your breath as you breath in, your body like a sun, and then the coolness as you breathe out, your flow like a moon. Imagine a deep blue sky all around you, and a moon in the sky, and a sun within you, as you flow between these two forces.' I could feel Hana breathing next to me, also lying on her mat and blankets, and then her breathing aligned with mine. Adrian hit one of the sound bowls and the warm sound reverberated outwards, filling the room; my mind filled with amber.

'Breathe in deeply, mindful of the sun within, and then hold for two seconds. And then breathe out. And then hold for two seconds again. And then breathe in, and consider what memories emerge as you breathe, warm and cold memories, gentle and painful memories – but then hold, retain, and let go. Breathe out. You are bleeding thoughts into the cosmos; the room can contain them all, and then the sky, and then the universe. Don't resist their movement. Let them rise and disappear.'

As Adrian said these things, he kept beating the sound bowl, and new vibrations would echo around; as he suggested memories, they emerged, as if he had called them into being, like tiny chasing demons. A memory of my father, first, unconscious. His cheeks pink with fever. A pain in my chest, that I was losing him.

'Breathe in, and let the pain linger and spread – and then out – and it is gone. Remember to let it go. If it comes back, let it go again.' And yet as he said this, and I kept breathing, I didn't want to let it go. With every breath, I hung on, savouring the crystalline pain, the last attachment.

We breathed more and Adrian spoke less, but he moved around, and I could feel his presence. He placed one of the metal bowls on my chest and I felt its weight on my heart; each breathe felt somehow more indulgent for its effort and I found the weight comforting. After a few deep breaths, he drummed another bowl over my head, sending vibrations through my chest, my spine, my hips. I breathed out, anticipating another, and after a moment he beat it again. My body responded to the vibrations, relaxing, and I lingered in its release.

'Good,' he said, pounding the golden bowl once more before moving on to Hana.

I drifted off as he played more of these bowls like reverbed organ music, whilst wafting incense around. It was the same as the incense in Mass, warm and clinging and smoky, frankincense and myrrh. I breathed it in greedily, filling my lungs, holding it, and letting it escape me again. Only then did I notice Hana was asleep, because she was snoring; Adrian banged a sound bowl over her head, though, and she stirred and awoke.

Adrian spoke again as he played, the frequency of the sound increasing, the lights dimming to a slow glow.

'Your pain is a blessing,' he said, 'lean into it. Let it burn you gently to ashes so that you can be reborn.' As he said this, I imagined Joan of Arc, the flames lapping at her hair, and disappearing into it. I opened my eyes, and I was cold; I wrapped the blanket closer around me.

'Keep going,' he said. I saw Hana twitch next to me, rearranging herself. 'Breathe out, let your memories back into the world, let yourself disappear.' I closed my eyes again and imagined the ash being blown away into a cascade of stars, disappearing.

Adrian started singing, then - a guttural, wordless hymn. When he was finished, he told us to sit up and open our eyes. He handed us each one of the bowls, and a wooden mallet.

'You can now bring this around the rim of the bowl,' he said, 'very slowly. Like this. Be gentle, remember.' He was looking at Hana as he said this, and she did as she was told, and a low whimper emerged as she did so, getting louder. I did the same, and these sounds flowed into one another in an anarchic harmony, soft and sultry, as the shadows from the candles lapped the walls.

Adrian came over and wafted some more of the incense around and then got his own mallet and hit it against a massive gong, sending sound waves through our space.

'Let them rest,' he said, and we put the bowls down. He came over to me and laid his hands over my face very gently and said 'good,' and then moved over to Hana and said, 'very good, Hana,' and then went and sat back at his own mat. 'Let's sit now for a moment to reflect and bring ourselves back into the present moment. We have been reborn, and we have done this together.'

We folded up our blankets and moved towards the door, and when Adrian opened it, light flooded in. I went downstairs, slightly dazed, and smiled when I saw Nate, until I saw that Sacha, a friend of Adrian who had arrived not long before me, was lying in his lap, and his hand was resting on her head, his other hand on her bare shoulder. Adrian saw my reaction and put his own arm around me, but I felt limp with the shock.

'Come on,' Adrian said, 'let's all have a nice time, okay?' Nate moved Sacha off his lap and lit a cigarette as if nothing had happened. Adrian put some music on. I stayed with Hana, though this time we did not clean up or cook together, but sat close in the tan leather sofa, sharing cigarettes. We stayed there, barely talking but just listening to the music, until the others left. I saw Nate disappear soon after Sacha, and I tried not to care, not to feel a certain frustration at the tedious repetition of these things.

'Have you seen any of the researchers when you've been cleaning their station lately?' Hana asked me, distracting me from my resentment.

'No,' I said. 'Hardly ever. But they come back and forth, I think. I still keep all the data for them anyway. Are they supposed to be there all the time? I thought maybe they had gone on their holidays.'

Hana looked at me for a moment and then sighed. 'I don't think that's the reason. I think they are avoiding the birds.' I thought about what she meant by this; whenever I had seen any of them in person, they had kept their distance, but then they had always been quite aloof, so it didn't seem that odd.

Now that Hana mentioned it though, I hadn't seen them

in person in about a fortnight; I had been continuing with my research, but I had been saving it on a shared document and we had never met to discuss it. They had never raised the alarm as such, though I knew better than anyone that the death tolls were rising. But I thought of this pattern like a tide coming in; it was a natural occurrence, as Nate had said. Eventually the tide would go out again. We could just not enjoy the beaches so well until that happened. But the island did not exist merely for our leisure.

'Do you think we should be avoiding them as well then? More than we are, I mean? The birds?'

Hana looked away then, at the fire that was still burning, though nearly gone to ash. The log was glowing with the last of its heat.

'I think perhaps Nate and Adrian are not being as transparent about the problem as they could be. I don't think they want to leave the island. They are so attached to it.'

'Nate would never leave the island. He loves it here.'

'Well exactly. But we should be able to make that decision for ourselves; they can't decide everything. Especially not something like that. I nearly went for a swim today you know, in the lagoon. But even from the shore I could see about ten dead birds floating there. I couldn't believe I had even considered swimming; how in denial I had been. I couldn't believe I hadn't asked more questions.'

'I can ask Nate if you like?'

'No, don't do that,' Hana replied, wearily. 'Don't tell him I've said any of this. I don't want to cause a drama.'

'But isn't that the problem? We've been complacent, not asking questions. When maybe we should have.'

'I know, but the way Nate and Adrian have been recently, I don't really trust them to tell the truth. And maybe they don't even know. Maybe the researchers have just abandoned us here. Maybe there isn't even a big problem, and the birds are no danger to us, and we're all doing all we can. It's not the only reason I'm feeling uneasy.'

※

Life in the commune became more strained after that conversation, the angst we all felt in different ways becoming more difficult to ignore, as if we could no longer contain the individual tensions and resentments. Hana and I did less cooking, so the others grazed on the supplies, and we ran out more quickly. The boat trips were cancelled every other day because of staff shortages, and though Hana and I didn't talk about it again, I could see panic flash over her every time Adrian announced another delay or postponed trip.

We all ignored the birds, playing music louder and lighting candles and fires. Nate was meant to be finishing a commission, amid all this, which was also stressing him out. If I suggested a break, he would get angry.

'Adrian says you're holding me back,' he would say. 'Adrian says you're too resistant, because of your trauma. Adrian says that until you submit to the energies of the group, you don't stand a chance of healing – and neither do I.'

None of it even made sense anymore; he knew I was annoyed about the anarchy of our romantic entanglement as much as any past trauma. He knew I was frustrated that we could no longer talk so freely, that something had changed between us after all. And I was upset that as these days went on, I recognised him less and less, as he pulled away from me and into himself, into another side I could not fathom, which he seemed to present as an affront.

'And is all the coke helping you heal? I didn't realise that was such an integral part of the psychedelic therapy.'

'It's helping me get through this day, Lena! Nothing and nobody else is! I have a deadline next week and everyone is useless in my life! I need to get this painting finished and packed up so that I can get some money in, so we can get more supplies in. Who do you think is paying for all the candles?!'

I let him get on with his work, but he would find my new friendship with Hana irritating as well, so we would go outside and attempt to relax in a small alcove by the dock. And yet Hana was also struggling, becoming increasingly paranoid about the birds. I began to think she was reacting badly to the mushroom tea, and her agitation was becoming contagious.

'Don't tell them;' she said when she cried, immediately putting on dark glasses, and waving away some sickly-looking cormorants. 'They will just make me do another ritual. I don't want to do another ritual. They are not helping me. I have lost myself in these rituals. I have also lost interest in them.' She did not seem very well at all.

That night, I had a dream where I was in a room in a castle and another woman – Joan of Arc from the vision earlier – was on the other side of the door, screaming at me and trying to break in, but I just kept trying to keep the door shut. Realising she was going to break in, I ran to the window, opened it and climbed down the castle, then ran towards the road. I climbed into a passing truck with a man and then woke up.

But Nate was not there, so I got up and went into the other room, where he was sitting on the sofa. I startled him and he looked at me angrily, not expecting that I would be there. He was smoking a pipe this time, surrounded by detritus, some glasses and papers and litter, a scattering of empty wraps.

'I had the weirdest dream,' I said, but he just he replied,

'Go back to sleep.' I didn't want to though; my eyes adjusted to the dim light, and I saw him more clearly.

'What are you doing?' I asked him sleepily, but he just stared at me furiously.

'Go to sleep, Lena. I'll be there soon. Just go back to bed.'

I did as I was told but hearing him rustling around, I couldn't fall back to sleep, so I took another sleeping pill, which gently knocked me out.

Nate woke before I did, or perhaps he had never slept to begin with, and he was playing Dusty Springfield in the living room. I was dazed and took a while to get out of bed; only the desire for fresh coffee compelled me to rise. I put on one of Nate's tee shirts and went into the living room, where he was dancing.

'I'm going to make coffee,' I said, 'do you want any?'

'Oh, I don't need any of that,' he laughed, 'but can you make some poached eggs? And toast. We need the energy! But not Gulls' Eggs, they're not allowed anymore,' he rambled on. 'We're not allowed the other eggs. Only the good eggs allowed. You're a good egg, aren't you?'

'Sure,' I said, still half asleep, and went into the kitchen as he kept dancing. I put the espresso pot on the stove and a pot with water, waited for both to start boiling. I heard Nate change the music, now to Bonobo, and when the eggs were ready, I brought everything through to the living room on a tray. The dining table was covered in papers and paraphernalia, so I placed the tray on the coffee table, though it was also cluttered with empty coke and beer cans, littered with wraps and skins and miscellaneous smudges and scraps.

'We should clean up after breakfast,' he said, noticing the struggle it took to find room to place the tray down. 'But first, let's eat!'

'You're in a good mood,' I replied, and he sat down and started eating.

'Nourishment,' he said. 'This is what I needed all along. Nourishment!'

I had a few bites of my food but immediately felt sick, and just had the coffee instead, pushing the plate to one side. The eggs, even if not connected to the birds on the island, began to nauseate me.

'You need to eat more,' Nate said, noticing this. 'Stop trying to lose weight. It's not healthy. We can't get sick, you know. We have to keep up our immunity!' I almost laughed as he said this but saw that he was being serious now. The paranoia had spread to him too.

I went to the sink and turned the tap on, started washing up. 'I'm going to have a shower, and then we can go.' he said. 'Meditation starts in an hour. We have to keep our spirits up!'

'Sure.' I said, lathering my hands, washing the uneaten eggs away, the bright yolk clinging to the surface of the plate.

Nate disappeared into the bedroom as I finished the dishes and then tidied up, and I could smell that he was smoking something – a tinny, soft, chemical smell – but after his mood the night before, I didn't want to say anything. What difference did it make anyway? He would not listen to me; it would cause conflict. And yet his behaviour confused me, the casual nature of these decisions, the unpredictability of it all, but mostly the way in which he seemed to make everything feel normal and logical, even though it was not.

I wondered if all along, he had decided this is how things would be, this is how things had to be, and so then I had to just fall in line, either accept him or leave – that was always the implication, whether it was cleaning up all the time or just not protesting the latest thing he was smoking, at 11 a.m. on a Sunday morning, or not asking questions about the sickness he was hiding.

I knew whenever I looked at him, when there was this pregnant silence and he glanced at me sternly and seriously, that it was this way or no way, he had made his decisions. It didn't matter if they were reckless ones; he always looked at me in a way that implied these were the right decisions, everything he did and said was right, there were no consequences, this was just how it would be.

And in a way, I wanted that to be true as well; I wanted him to be right. I wanted him to know best. That gaze, however delusional, was also deeply reassuring. And so my own gaze just said yes in a profound complicity, and so, I accepted, I was just as much to blame as he was.

※

The following day, I saw Hana again; this time we met in the ruin of the chapel. We sat inside, looking out through the arched windows at the gleaming North Sea; where the ocean met the sky, it dazzled with white reflections, seeming all the more luminous through the dark frame of the stone walls. Hana had brought a bottle of wine and two glasses, and we sat on a blanket I had brought with me. I was always amazed that we had enough alcohol, even as our food supplies decreased. The boats back and forth from the mainland seemed mostly to deliver to those needs; Nate and Adrian must have prioritised that, or else they had just stocked up so much previously. In any case, we drank.

I had hoped Hana would be in a better mood today, but if anything she looked sadder, and her face was drawn and pale in a way that suggested she had been crying.

'Look at us now, after all those good intentions,' she said, pouring me a glass of wine. 'We're teaching our sorrows to swim.'

I smiled and looked out through the window again at the sea that surrounded us. 'It is all so much bigger than us,' I said. 'We have to just go with it.'

'You sound as brainwashed as I once was,' she said tiredly. 'I don't mean that as an insult by the way. It's not that there's no truth in it.'

I noticed a sickly gull land on the top of one of the old walls, eyeing us curiously. I tried to ignore it though; surely their disease was not so bad that they wanted wine instead of fish now too?

'You seem more disillusioned than usual,' I replied. 'Are things okay with Adrian?' She seemed to be holding back tears again, or she was just very tired.

'He's talking about eating the birds, Lena. I don't think he is of sound mind. I don't think I am of sound mind either. I keep wanting to cry all the time. As much as I love it here, and I really do, I am just beginning to get sick, and I can't keep ignoring it.' She emptied her glass of wine and poured another, a pain in her voice now. 'I can't breathe here anymore, for all the fresh air. I want to stay so much, and I am scared to leave it because I love it, but I cannot stay. My own body won't let me. It is telling me to go.'

'I know,' I replied. 'I wish you wouldn't, but I know.'

We drank the rest of our wine together and I knew it was her last night, without her telling me specifically. If heartache is contagious, then I had caught it. Her pain ached in me as if it were my own, and then it was my own; her words had left a wound in me that would not be stitched up.

※

When we went over to the other cottage the following morning, we found out that Hana had left overnight. Adrian was beside himself, pacing around his cottage when we arrived, seething with rage and betrayal.

'What happened?' Nate asked.

'She had a meltdown and just left! There was no good reason. She just kept talking about the birds, always the birds. How she had to leave because it was depressing her, the birds. It made no sense at all. She's been here through two long winters, and she can't deal with a few birds dying? I told her it's nature, and then she just left. She wouldn't listen.'

As Nate consoled Adrian, I held back, not telling them about the message she had sent me earlier, which I cradled in my pocket.

'I'm sorry I couldn't say goodbye' she said. 'I had to get the first boat out. I can't stay here anymore; I hope you understand. I feel completely depleted by everything. I need to get away. Take care. Find me if you ever leave. I hope you do. I don't think it's healthy there anymore. xx'

I didn't show the others, and out of habit I went to the kitchen to start preparing lunch for later. Only as I started slicing bread did I realise fully the that only reason I had gone there was to see Hana and to be away from the others. I stopped cutting the bread after a couple slices, suddenly bereft, knowing exactly what Hana had been speaking of. Depletion. I imagined her leaving, and then I imagined her free. I imagined her healthy, in air fresher than here.

Just then, there was a crash from the other room, and I went to look; Adrian was furiously throwing old bottles and glasses at the concrete wall outside, in a rage. Even Nate flinched as he picked up a glass bowl and aimed it at the wall as well, sending tiny, jagged shards of glass airborne. The floor glittered with his destruction. He stood there as his tantrum quietened, a look of satisfaction, even contentment. He had had his morning release; he stretched, then folded his arms.

'Sorry guys,' he said. 'I'm just torn up about Hana.'

'Come on,' Nate said then, suddenly the voice of reason. 'Let's get you something to take the edge off.' They went to the furthest side of the cobble street, where there was less broken glass, and huddled together in discussion, little flickers of their lighter like a morse code, a tender SOS signal I couldn't fail to decipher.

'Why was Adrian being so aggressive?' I asked Nate later. 'It all seems a bit excessive, even for him.'

'Sometimes you love someone and at the same time you want to kill them,' Nate said. 'He is upset she has gone.' he added, as if that made sense of what he had said.

'Because he couldn't kill her?' I asked. 'That's terrible, Nate. No wonder she left.'

'Because he couldn't love her. He's upset because he couldn't love her. He didn't really have it in him. He couldn't get through to her, he couldn't keep her.'

He reached over and turned his light off then, and I turned into him, feeling his heart beating fast, breathing into him as if he might disappear at any moment.

※

In the morning, we awoke to the smell of burning. I knew immediately what had happened, simply because the scent was so familiar. Adrian was burning the birds' carcasses; a sickly barbecue on a summer's day.

Nate was in a deep sleep, having finally slept properly after so many days awake, and I had to wake him. As he stirred, I could see a recognition fall over him too, and with it a look of resignation.

'Shall we check on him?' I asked. Nate just nodded, murmured a yes.

Outside on the cobbled stones, Adrian had created a mountain of dead birds, arranged in a certain way, and they were alight. He was wearing the same Hawaiian shirt that he had been wearing all week and some khaki shorts, and he was still puffing on a red vape.

'You're awake!' he grinned. 'Take a seat, here.'

He directed us to a table and chairs he had brought outside, where Sacha and Jon were already sitting, with glazed expressions on their faces. I looked to Nate as he sat down awkwardly. Adrian had laid out plates and cutlery and water.

'I had an idea last night,' Adrian said, sitting down at the head of the table, 'when you had all gone to bed. I was thinking of the problem of our hunger, and the problem of the birds. And then I was thinking about a book I was reading, about the death meditation. How we need to really confront our own death before we can be free again. It got me thinking,' and he laid his vape down, sipped some water, calmer now, his blue eyes brightening. 'We have all been carrying the weight of the birds and their deaths – that's what Hana was always going on about. It's why she left. And to stop us all crumbling under the weight of their deaths, we have to confront it!' I looked at Nate and he was listening with interest. 'We need a ritual; we need to be nourished. These deaths have paralysed us, but they can nourish us if we want them too. Perhaps, after all, it's what nature intended?'

I wanted to argue that perhaps nature never intends anything, that perhaps we were disrupting nature, and perhaps in our meddling, we would sicken ourselves, just as we had disturbed the birds; as if a natural order would always win out. But I was too weak to speak up, to voice my concerns. He went on.

'We need to protect ourselves,' Adrian said. 'From the fear that has been rising in us. This is the perfect chance for a rebirth. But first, we eat!'

I looked around the table, at Sacha and Jon, who had barely spoken in weeks, and Nate, who seemed shut down to me now, ignoring my gaze. Adrian brought over some charred birds and laid them on the table. He had obviously gone to some effort, but they did not look appetising. As he carved into the bird, I remembered the dinner with Nate a couple weeks ago, and I wondered again if what we had eaten back then had been chicken, or if it had been one of these fallen, sick birds, if this death ritual had been going on for some time. I looked at Nate as he was handed a plate, which he handed to me. I did not ask him; I knew he would not answer, whatever I said.

'Eat up, friends!' Adrian said, and then Nate turned to smile at me, like a little boy in a game. He took a forkful of the breast and held it to my mouth.

'Open up,' he said. As I did so, I could feel the other birds looking at us, and I thought of Hana, and I wished I had been strong enough to follow her before it got to this.

As Jon said a prayer for the birds and for the cycle of life, for being purged of fear, for our immunity, the meat settled in my stomach. I looked beyond the hill to the ocean and wished to be in it, alive or dead, rather than here.

9

THOUGH THERE WERE many things that were concerning, it was really the marathon sound bath afternoon that pushed me over the edge. Adrian had lined up psychically relevant sound bowls throughout the house and had a complex schedule that everyone had agreed to observe, following twelve hours of fasting. The group convened in the main space of the building, where Adrian and Nate had arranged all the mats and blankets, with the bowls in the centre.

When I sat down on my allocated mat, Adrian handed me a small metal bowl and a mallet and I started moving it around the edge like I had before, but this time there were no vibrations and no sound. Adrian noticed.

'Try tucking your thumb underneath, so it is just resting on your palm,' he said. But that didn't help. 'Try holding the mallet differently,' he said, and he moved my hand with his. But it still didn't work, and he grew concerned. 'There are no vibrations at all,' he said. 'No vibrations, Lena.' He looked disappointed and moved away. I kept trying, but there was no sound from the singing bowl.

Then we all lay down again and Adrian went through the meditation and played the bowls, but instead of feeling relaxed, I began to feel claustrophobic. I kept thinking of Aidan, this time, and imagining him with the gallerist; then I thought of Nate, remembering when he had mentioned other women to taunt me during sex, then how he had looked at me the next day. I remembered

Hana and wished she were here. I understood, intently, why she had gone, and now I wanted to go too. I closed my eyes, and tried to meditate to the others' sounds, to bring myself back to them, but something stopped me connecting; as they swelled around me, the singing bowls chiming with the gulls and the sea, I had a sense that if I kept listening, I would drown in the noise, as if my consciousness were being colonised by the island's sounds, by Nate, by everyone here – by some amorphous contagion that perhaps I had been naïve to welcome so easily, to want to be contained in. I had once felt this submission to the sounds as a freedom, but now it seemed to threaten me, and without thinking it through at all, without knowing what I was about to do, I said, 'no,' and opened my eyes.

I sat up then; everyone else still had their eyes closed, lying on their mats. Adrian did as well but he must have sensed my movement as he opened his eyes and looked at me. I signalled that I was going to go but he shook his head sternly. I got up anyway, folding my blanket, and moved towards the door. Adrian stood up, and the singing bowls stopped vibrating and echoing, and yet no one else opened their eyes. I went towards the door, but Nate got up from his mat and blocked me.

'This is a chance to grow,' Nate whispered angrily, and I could sense eyes upon us now. 'You just have to stay put. You're resisting because you're not open enough, but all you have to do is lie down and breathe and let the resistance pass.' He said all of this so intensely that it angered me; it seemed so ridiculous to say these things.

'But I can't today,' I said. 'I've done this so many times now, but today I don't want to. I need some fresh air.' I went to move but he grabbed my arm firmly and stopped me.

'You're too resistant!' He was shouting now, and wouldn't let go of my arm, so I resisted more. 'You have to trust the process, or it won't work. You have to be open to connection.' He still wouldn't let go of my arm, and now held me with his other arm as well.

'No! This isn't going to work anymore. I don't want it anymore. This isn't freedom, and that's becoming more and more obvious. That's why Hana left. You're a tyrant, this project is tyrannical, and I'm sick of it!' At that, he finally let go and looked at me with a depth of hatred I had never seen in him before.

'Then leave.' I was shocked when he said this, and immediately a part of me didn't want to anymore, but I could not backtrack now.

'I am. I am leaving.' I said, more quietly now. I could see the rest of the group looking at me as well, with their dark, blank expressions. I could hear the dying gulls in the background, as ever, and the hissing waves, and all of a sudden I did not feel the belonging I once had.

'Leave now.' he said.

'I am leaving now.' I turned and opened the door and did not look back, at least not while he could see me. I went back to the cottage, packed my things all at once into the overnight bag I'd arrived with, and made my way to the harbour, trying to ignore the cries of the sick gulls and cormorants, the dying puffins, the old skeleton wings lying all around in the grass and the bracken.

I felt tears, then; I had been so afraid of the birds and the death they carried with them, that without even realising it, I had not cried for them until now. I had not cried for all the fallen birds, their bones scattered all over the island we had briefly shared, their island.

When I got to the dock, my tears dried as I waited two hours until a boat came. It was lucky it came at all, and even then, the captain didn't want to let me on.

'This is just a delivery boat,' he said, in his gruff way. 'I'm just delivering food and then leaving.'

'I can't stay anymore,' I said. 'I'm not sick, I just have to leave. I was here to do research and now it's time to go.' He seemed to accept my vague pragmatism, and I made sure to communicate none of the panic I now felt, the desperation to get on the boat.

'You can sit at the back then,' he said. 'You're lucky it's a peaceful day today. The weather has been dire this week.'

'I know,' I said. 'So many cancelled boats.'

He looked at me sternly, but said nothing, and I sat tight as the boat left the shore, leaving the gulls on the rocks, and my friends in their own colony, and once again I experienced the bliss I had come here for, the bliss of escape. As we sailed all around the island, past its charcoal grey cliffs smattered with white, past the caves and alcoves, indigo-grey waves rolling against their shores, I forgot myself in its beauty, the depth of its magic.

And though I knew I had to leave, I knew I would never know somewhere quite so sublime, an island whose presence was so powerful and all-consuming that I had felt I was a part of it, rather than a separate human, whilst I had been there. And as soon as I had gone too far, as soon as it became something on the horizon rather than my home, I missed it more than ever.

10

SIX MONTHS LATER

THE WINTER LIGHT began to fade late afternoon. It was the winter solstice, and Hana mixed me a special lemonade with crushed ice in a crystal glass; the reflections of the candles on the dinner table danced in the windows as the inky sky gradually enveloped us. I was here to see the painting, which was almost finished, before she went away for Christmas.

'This way,' she said, and I followed her, bringing the drink with me. We went into her dining room, where she was storing all her work for now. The painting was very little and still on the easel. 'It's not completely dry yet,' she said. 'It'll take a few more weeks. If I don't decide to change it again. But I think it's done.'

I moved closer, standing about three feet from the canvas. It was just me sitting by a window, wearing black and looking distant. 'It's strange that I look like I am in other world, when I was trying so hard to be present.'

She laughed dismissively. 'Oh, that's okay, that's not your fault at all. You were very good. You just have an ethereal look about you sometimes, that's all. And I was daydreaming too; the artist always projects onto the model.'

I kept looking closer, remembering the light as I had felt it then, trying to match it up with how it looked now. The room was mostly in shadow, though, a blueish haze, with my skin and hands lit up by that wan afternoon light. I did not exactly recognise myself, though I could see that she had achieved a likeness. But she had captured something else, too – as she said, her own daydreams, her own mood, and the feeling of those hazy afternoons, which I had felt too.

'I love it,' I said, 'this deep pulsing blue.' She had managed to achieve the impression of the ocean, somehow, of being underwater, surrounded by waves enveloping us gently.

'Thank you,' she said. 'I'm glad you like it. Thank you for sitting all those times.'

'It was like a long meditation,' I replied. 'It was good for me too. I'm just glad you got something of use before you had to leave.'

'I'm so relieved you got out in time too,' she said. 'I was so shocked when I heard they had closed the island completely.' I had been too, of course; when the researchers found that the bird disease could spread to humans, they had shut it off entirely, and the others had been forced to stay in the Colony indefinitely; though Hana and I agreed that they probably would have stayed there regardless, they were so committed to their life there.

For a time, I was worried that the researchers would track me down too, in their determination to keep the disease contained, but I kept a low profile, and they never did. I got in touch with Hana, as she had asked me to, when she left, and she was doing the same.

We had not spoken very much about it, though; it was anxiety inducing to go into too many details, so we avoided that. Instead, we talked about the portrait, our own little project that, I hoped, had resisted the influence of the Colony, and so become our small rebellion. In my romantic moments, I thought that in some way, it had saved us. We had merged together in this thing; we had become light and colour, a portal into this new life.

We moved back into the kitchen again; it was dark and the lights danced in the windows.

'Isn't it strange how different everything feels now.' I said. 'It really wasn't all that long ago. I was like another person, then. You were too.'

'Well, here you can just be yourself again,' she said, ignoring any reference to herself, and I was confused for a moment. 'You were just doing what you were told back then,' she went on. 'So you couldn't really just be yourself.'

'I thought I was being, though. During the sittings at least. I was just in my own thoughts so much of the time. But we talked as well, and I liked that.'

'Yes, but now you can speak and move around more freely, away from the island and Nate's influence. And even mine. Sitting for a portrait is an unnatural thing.' I was surprised that her tone was quite harsh now, and she did indeed seem like a new person. 'You are in one pose for such a long time. There aren't many times in life that anyone sits still for that long.'

She topped up my lemonade then, which I wanted to enjoy but did not, because I kept imagining vodka in it, and she sat down across from me.

'But you were telling me that I should slow down,' I said, 'that I should be still.'

'And you were, but you had me telling you to do it. Perhaps if you could embrace your own self-control, do it for yourself, and not for someone else. But maybe this is a start.'

Hana's words irritated me then, though I tried not to show it. But she noticed anyway. 'I'm not trying to criticise you,' she said. 'Or tell you another thing to do – it's not meant like that.'

'I know. But it does make me feel, more generally, that nothing I do is enough. Whether I tell myself to be still or you do or someone else does. Or the opposite. It is still just pressure. And it is a lonely sort of pressure. I keep coming back to this – that nothing is enough.' I had not known I had felt it about her too until she told me I had just been following orders, and deficient in that way. Until her mood had dampened my own.

'I'm sorry,' she replied, her voice lower now. 'It's not what I meant. I'm sorry . . . I'm not communicating myself very well.' As her guard fell then, I warmed to her again.

'You don't need to be sorry; I understand what you're saying, and why. It's just how I feel. It's not about you. You've been kind.' I sensed that both of us were confused now and wish I had said nothing.

Hana sat down opposite me then, fidgeting and fractious. My immediate instinct was to leave, and yet I didn't want to leave, because it would prolong whatever this was. Pain, that is what it was.

'I know you were having a hard time,' she said, looking at me directly now. 'And I'm sorry I couldn't do more to help. I'm sorry I had to leave when I did.' She reached over and touched my hand, but I couldn't bear it; I pulled my hand away, suddenly wanting to cry, aware all at once how miserable we had both been. I had romanticised our time together, and yet seeing Hana now, still struggling, brought back the heaviness we had both brought from the island to our new lives. It was too much; perhaps alone we could ignore it, but together it was inescapable.

'I'm sorry,' I said. 'I have to go.' I started to move, I took my bag, but she looked at me sternly.

'Don't go,' she said. I stopped what I was doing, and stayed there, and then wiped my eyes. The dynamic had not changed; I still did as I was told, as if I were still her model.

'I'm sorry,' I said again.

'Please stop saying sorry.' She sounded frustrated; I noticed she had removed her hand from the table now too.

'I just had a bad week,' I tried to explain. 'I'm trying to figure things out. It's not easy to do, giving up everything.' Hana relaxed as I said this, perhaps because she felt less powerless now, perhaps because she could tell me what I could do again.

'Do you think you might go back to therapy?' she asked me, with a brighter tone. 'It can be so helpful, especially after everything we went through.'

I felt uncomfortable as she suggested this, remembering the island again. I thought we had an unspoken agreement not to tell anyone else about it; that our history was ours alone, contained and precious. And yet I wanted to agree with her; I did want to change as well. I wanted to trust other people again, other strangers.

'I might go back,' I said.

'I've found it so helpful myself,' she went on. 'And you don't have to keep going if you don't want to. But it's worth trying, in case it helps this time.' I bristled as she said this; a part of me resented being told, however subtly, that I might need help or that something so quotidian as therapy might be the fix. And yet this was strange too; I kept turning to Hana, and other people before her, after bad situations, breakups, crashes and so on, and yet when she asked if I needed help, my instinct was to say no, and to shrug off reasonable suggestions. I wanted a more exciting solution than that.

'I find it hard . . .' but I couldn't find the words, trailed off. 'I think perhaps I like to believe I am just fleetingly involved in chaos that is a result of bad luck rather than bad decisions. Or even worse, my own abdication of decisions to another person.'

'Well, if you admitted to making bad decisions,' she replied, 'then you might have to make different ones. If you admitted handing over your agency to other people, you might start doubting that way of life.'

'I know,' is all I could say, but I could see now that she knew everything there was to know about me already, and she had been studying me just as I had sunken into her easy shelter. This is why she had just let me hang around when things were going badly, being part of the furniture, as she would say back then. And I did want to be part of the furniture; I wanted nothing more than to be reduced to an inanimate object, and she had kindly made that possible. When I had been with her, I had just existed in a reduced, easy way, and she had not criticised me for it, not questioned it particularly, not taken advantage.

How daunting though, to have to be a person now, when I had for so long taken solace in being a thing. Somehow, having finally been turned into an actual object – this painting – some spell had been broken though. I could no longer keep going on in this way, being a mere thing, pretending to be a thing. The object – the painting – had been achieved.

I could not really compete with it. By seeing the painting, it had been revealed to me that I was not actually just a thing, or rather, it was better at being a thing than I was. I would now be forced out of my stillness; I would have to blink. I would have to breathe. I would have to become fully conscious. The thought sickened me, but I could not avoid the transformation any longer.

As the days went on in this languorous stretch of time, immediate and hazy at once, I did not enjoy being conscious; it was painful. My thoughts and sensations stretched out beyond my control, and yet even as it hurt, I wanted it. I had always thought before that I felt too much, and that was why I wanted to contain it all so much. And yet now I felt and hurt and needed and wanted, but I had to let it be. I had no one and nothing to constrain me, only this overwhelming, terrifying freedom. I had been scared of this, of all this, and for good reason.

And yet as it hurt, as it enveloped me, I tried to love life as much as I had once loved men, I tried to tolerate life as much as I had tolerated men. I tried to love the mainland as I had once loved the island. The commitment I had so wanted all this time was here at last; it was not to one man, though, but all men, all of myself, all of life. I would spread the good news. No wonder I had tried to close myself into one bottle and one tight embrace. And yet to be born I had to leave that closed space; it had gone on too long, this strange pregnancy, and if I did not leave then it would smother me, it would kill me, I would die before I lived.

※

After seeing the portrait and leaving Hana, a frustration began to hang over me. At first, I blamed my new sobriety, but as the days went on, I could only blame it for allowing me to feel everything, including frustration, more clearly. Though Hana had held me in this dynamic in a kind way, I started thinking she had done so partly to show me what I had been doing compulsively for years – giving myself over to other people, putting myself in a space in which I did not have to have any control.

I had only been sitting there but in those hours, she had control, and I had found peace in her having control. As soon as the portrait was finished though, that arrangement also ended, and in a way, it had resulted in the end point of this dynamic – becoming an object. I had disappeared into it, as usual; Hana had projected her own feelings onto me so that she could complete the work. I had been her mirror, too.

The frustration gave way to a simpler, softer pain. Hana was gone and I stopped talking. I looked back at my own picture of her painting, and I couldn't really see myself in it. I could only see her. And in relationships, other people and I had also projected our desires onto each other so that we could complete the project of escaping ourselves. We were stuck in this avoidant dance, never quite connecting, and yet producing, always producing. I had done so much work. I had so many moments I could remember, memories of sensations, and yet they had gone, the bodies had gone, I had gone. Only work remained.

Masochism made love impossible in the end; it required too much repression. But it produced work. I had let myself be destroyed for the sake of the project – these relationships, the projects – until I had broken apart. And then, seeing me broken, they would always leave. 'I want something light and fun, and this is not that.' And I would go back to work.

I had for so long romanticized my own compulsions, partly because their nature was also romantic; I began thinking somehow that I could find freedom in spinning around in these loops. But I had only found misery – repeating the people I loved, becoming a mere echo of them. Narcissus and Echo were one and the same; they and I were one and the same. I had dissolved into this odd dance with them, the false transcendence of oblivion. My voice disappeared to an echo and only came back when I was in Mass, for want of anything better to do, where I gravitated towards again.

If I spoke in there, it was only to echo the Priest's words – Peace be with you / and also with you / Amen / Amen / Pray for us sinners now, and at the hour of our death – and yet the more I repeated of this, and the more it physically resonated – the chant and the ideas at once – the calmer I became. So many years looking for love in men; but if I had not tried, had not lived that way, had not loved them, or tried to – then I never would have found this other love, a desire for life itself, not a merely a mirrored descent. Life had become so small and desperate, and yet the desperation, I was told, was a gift.

And yet first the anger, the immense anger I now felt. I was still not as old as Tristan had been when we had a relationship, when I was still a teenager. I was nearly a decade younger than he had been when we met, still. And in every relationship since, I had been battling this shame, turning the anger in on myself, self-medicating it all away. Finding new men who were just the same, and hoping somehow that they would not hurt me just the same as he had. And then he had died of an overdose, and I had been trying to escape from that ever since. I had been taking pictures ever since, too, removing myself from the present in such an intentional way. But it was crushing me, this reliance on a parallel world, the basic unreality of it all. The men in my life: none of them were here now. I was mostly alone; they had disappeared like vapour, a magic trick, a sudden death repeated over and over again.

I had not slept peacefully of my own volition for about five years, but I could see that I might be freed from that need if I could be awake to life now, if I could just stay awake. When the insomnia was bad, my thoughts would spiral and my heart would beat too fast; then flashbacks would all come back, dragging me down into a lucid hellscape of past lives. Some nights, I stayed awake for it all, but I would feel wounded from it. I would cry myself to sleep, other times, only wanting death in those moments. One memory kept returning to me, as those nights went on: I remembered that I had my first drink when I had just turned nine, when I'd been sent to stay with cousins while my father was in hospital having his cancerous kidney removed.

I had gone to France with them on my ninth birthday, having just said goodbye to my father in hospital, and I cried every day for two weeks. But the family friend I was staying with just shouted at me if I cried, saying it was pathetic I wanted to call home every day – and then these teenagers, a bit older than me, told me to drink the wine instead. All these years later, and I was there again – in a room by myself, having been shouted at to stop crying, to stop being difficult – to have a drink instead.

Except that I didn't even want a drink; I hadn't then, and I didn't now. I had wanted to cry, and I still did. That woman shouting at me had just been replaced by men shouting, one after another; my sick father had been replaced by them too. And the French teenagers drifted on in my life perpetually, this forming and reforming commune. Here I was again. And yet I was no longer nine years old, and those people had gone. And those men had gone (they were always going). And then at last I could go, too. I was always leaving, too.

When I did give up the sleeping pills a final time, and I could sleep again, it seemed miraculous. I had not thought it remotely possible for so many years; I had been living in this state of perpetual anxiety. But the pills had been feeding the anxiety and the claustrophobia, and the repression of all my painful reactions, and I only really understood that when I stopped taking them, stopped letting them take me.

Even though I slept badly for some time after returning from the island, I was still more awake the next day than I had been before. It was only then that I realised the degree to which I had been sleepwalking, gradually losing my consciousness, so that I was asleep to life. Past relationships now seemed like strange dreams, in which things from reality were confused and distorted, fears were blown up, sensations amorphous and deceptive, addicting. I had not been awake; I had been living in various states of unconsciousness.

There were not many people in attendance at Mass the night before Christmas, and I sat a few rows behind the altar. To my right there was a large statue of Saint Michael, the archangel in armour, holding his sword defiantly, prised to defeat Satan. A few yards behind him there was Mary, with rows of candles in front of her in a black iron tray, offering penance to sinners. Some candles had burnt out and a few were lit. There was a box of fresh candles ready to be used. For now, I sat in my wooden pew and waited.

It was so dark outside that the stained-glass windows were cast in its gloom, so I looked instead at the paintings hooked to the stone walls – Jesus carrying his cross, Mary with Jesus. To the left of the altar, a little chapel with more seats around its edges, and candles lit. In my way, I had been trying to forgive for years. Photography had been one avenue; with each image I attempted to humanise and then detach those whose presence in my mind tormented me. But the resentment rose up, like it had recently, and I felt like a child left unsoothed.

I went to the tray of candles and lit several at once – one for each boyfriend – and as I did so I was comforted by the large Saint Michael looming down on me. As I let the flames lick the white wax, I felt that at the heart of my difficulty in forgiving them was actually a concern for them. For people to behave badly, there is always pain; I had behaved that way too. That shared pain was hard to let go of. But now I tried to give that worry away. These men were no longer my concern, and yet everyone was my concern. Love was at the heart of forgiveness, but also a reason I struggled to forgive. How to reconcile love with abuse? How to accept the complexity of other people and myself? How to just leave and go on?

Forgiveness is a little death; it requires an acknowledgement of how things really were, what someone really did. It requires the acceptance of a painful, splintering reality. It was therefore an ending of one stretch of life, one belief, one hope. But it was also freedom from the bondage of loving someone specifically and personally, and the embrace of a more universal concern and care. It was the breaking of an intimate bond and finding freedom in that severing of ties.

And what could be more loving than that? The love was heightened in becoming universal, in transcending the particularity of one bond. There is a shared vulnerability in being hurt by someone else; you see them at their weakest, and they see you at your weakest. In a way, who hurt whom is beside the point: both people are confronted by human weakness, by this mutual failure to be connected, in that moment, by anything but shared pain.

Every night, I prayed for my friends on Gull Island, that they would survive the outbreak as I had, and as Hana had, and that they would be truly free one day. It had been a miracle, really, that we had got out alive, and seemed to be symptom free. I kept a low profile, as Hana did too. We both knew that containment couldn't work anyway; that birds could fly, and as such, they could spread their disease. And this did happen – all over the East Coast. First of all, the birds began to fall, their bones washing up on otherwise pristine shores. It was only a matter of time before some people started to fall, too. And when it got to the humans it seemed cataclysmic; the terror spread just by touching, breathing, even talking. Just by being together.

It did occur to me, sometimes, that Hana or I might have spread it, that one of us may even have been patient zero, as it were. When they tried to stop the spread, as it later grew so out of hand, we knew it was already too late. We had seen miracles; we were proof that it was possible to live through it all and feel freer than ever on the other side. They could never have contained the island, our little colony, for long; for better and worse the ideas and infections spread, as nature intended, and we could only be grateful to survive it.

Acknowledgements

I AM INCREDIBLY thankful to Chris, Jennifer, and Kirsty at Salt Publishing for their warmth, kindness and support in publishing The Colony (and particularly for Chris' patience with my many minor adjustments!) I am also deeply grateful to my agent Tom Cull, who has been so lovely to work with from the very beginning.

Thank you to friends who read very early versions of this novel or writing that somehow informed the final work, especially Cian McCourt, Luke Brown, and Charlie Gilmour. Thank you also to Joshua Press for inviting me to sit for a portrait a few winters ago, which inspired me to write about that process in another setting.

Lastly, thank you to my son Caspian, who accompanied me on a trip to the Isle of May, off the coast of Fife, where this story crystallised the moment we stepped ashore, and we heard the eerie cries of thousands of birds.

This book has been typeset by
SALT PUBLISHING LIMITED
using Neacademia, a font designed by Sergei Egorov for the
Rosetta Type Foundry in Czechia. It has been manufactured
using Holmen Book Cream 65gsm paper, and printed and
bound by Clays Limited in Bungay, Suffolk, Great Britain.

CROMER
GREAT BRITAIN
MMXXVI